BOUND

FALLEN WORLD SERIES BOOK 1

C.R. JANE

MILA YOUNG

Bound

C. R. Jane & Mila Young

Bound by C. R. Jane and Mila Young

Copyright © 2019 by C. R. Jane and Mila Young

For permissions contact:

crjaneauthor@gmail.com

milayoungauthor@gmail.com

This book is a work of fiction. Names, characters, businesses, places, events, locales, and incidents are either the products of the author's imagination or used in a fictitious manner. Any resemblance to actual persons, living or dead, or actual events is purely coincidental.

Cover by Everly Yours Cover Design

❀ Created with Vellum

To anyone who ever looked up at the stars and dreamed.

Join C.R. Jane's Readers' Group

Stay up to date with C.R. Jane by joining her Facebook readers' group, C.R.'s Fated Realm. Ask questions, get first looks at new books/series, and have fun with other book lovers!

Join Mila Young's Readers' Group

Join Mila Young's Wicked Readers Group to chat directly with Mila and other readers about her books, enter giveaways, and generally just have loads of fun!

Join Mila Young's Readers' Group

Bound

They came to Earth. They destroyed my life, took those closest to me, and now they're set on making me their own.

Ella Monroe has only one goal in life. To survive. Trapped in a world that's been taken over, Ella is reminded daily of everything that she has lost because of the Vepar. What was supposed to be a fun night out to celebrate her birthday turns into a nightmare encounter at a Vepar club when she catches the eye of three terrifyingly alluring men.

Powerful and terrifyingly seductive, the three Vepar make clear they will stop at nothing to possess her. Unable to escape, Ella is plunged into their dangerous and secretive world, where everything is more than it seems. Ella doesn't know what the future holds as their prisoner, but one thing is for sure. Their obsession knows no bounds...

PROLOGUE

They came in the night. There were no gunshots fired. No one's last breath was given for their kingdom or country. It was just over. And they were in charge. They told us that our governments had no choice...that they did what was best for us by giving in. As I watched the President and the First Lady be frog marched out the front gates of the White House by a group of their armed guards, the President and his wife with just one bag in each of their hands, it was clear to see that life as we knew it would never be the same again.

Years later, I would think back on that moment and wonder if that was the first time I had seen them. If they somehow sensed even then that I was out there and that I was something that they would want...something they would obsess over. I wondered if there was anything I could have done, any way that I could have run to ensure a different outcome.

It didn't do any good for me to think about what-ifs. The simple fact of the matter was that I was never given a choice. I belonged to them. I always would.

1

iar!

"I didn't steal the money," I whispered to Greg to avoid the customers in the diner from hearing our conversation. Biting back the fury that danced through me, I curled my hands and stuffed them into the pockets of my skirt, concealing them. How dare he accuse me of theft after I'd worked here for the past year and covered every necessary shift, stayed until midnight to close up most nights, and even cooked the damn food when we were short on staff. I stared at my boss in disbelief. He may only be five foot three and sporting a shaved haircut to cover his receding hairline, but he reminded me of a bulldog with his squished nose, chubby cheeks, and downturned mouth. His brown eyes squinted in an accusatory manner.

"You were responsible for the register," he barked, not caring that he was raising his voice.

My cheeks burned, and I opened my mouth to respond, but no words formed. I *was* the only waitress on hand today because Sandy called in sick, again, and was most likely having a full day of orgasms with her new boyfriend. *Lucky her.* The cooks couldn't have touched the cash since they never came up front. So that left me...

I exhaled loudly. "I know it looks that way, but it wasn't me. You know me, Greg. You know I wouldn't do that to you." I wished he'd installed cameras as I suggested months ago. Then we wouldn't be having this problem.

Greg huffed, his shoulders rising and falling. "The lost money will come out of your next check."

"No!" I reached out for him, but he batted me away, scrunching his nose as if I were no better than a fly.

"That's a douche move, man," Cherry's voice came behind me, my best friend who often came here for lunch and to bug me. She meant well, but this would only get worse if she tried to interfere.

I turned towards her and shook my head, mouthing the word, *don't.*

She ignored me and climbed out of the nearby booth located right behind the register and strolled toward us in her stilettos. "She's innocent until proven guilty. So, you can't dock Ella's pay without evidence."

Greg stood as tall as he was able, his hands gripping his wide hips, his name badge sitting at an angle across his heart. The corners of his lips twitched in distaste as he looked at my best friend. "My diner. My rules. You don't like it, both of you can leave." His voice rose and I realized that the rest of the diner had fallen silent, listening to our argument.

"Well," Cherry began, but I stepped in front of her.

"It's fine." My heart raced at the thought of losing my job when I was already living paycheck to paycheck. "I'll cover the missing money."

Cherry exhaled loudly behind me, while Greg just grinned.

"That was never a question," he replied snottily before he turned and marched into the back office.

"Fucking ass," Cherry murmured as she snatched my elbow to drag me to sit in the cushioned booth with her. "He can kiss my ass, that dick is lucky to have you working for him." She pushed over her half-eaten vegetable fries and I helped myself, deciding I might as well drown my sorrows in food. But the food didn't sit well in my stomach with all the worry that was churning through me. It also didn't help that I still remembered how real French fries tasted, and this "healthier" version couldn't compare.

I tucked the loose strands of hair behind my ear, but it was a losing battle as it fell right back into my face. "I'm going to lose half my pay, and after paying rent, I'll have nothing left to live off this month," I told her as I gloomily stuck another disgusting vegetable fry into my mouth.

I looked outside the diner window to the blue sky that was growing heavier with clouds. There was supposed to be a storm rolling in tonight and the sky was certainly starting to look foreboding. Just as I had that thought the sound of thunder boomed from outside sending a shiver down my spine. My grandma had always warned me that thunder was an omen, but I'd never given much weight to such supernatural tales. Not when my life was work, earn enough to pay my rent, and save enough for a car.

I sighed again. I was never going to be ahead. I had dreams once upon a time for how my life was going to be. They certainly didn't involve working at the Cinnamon Diner forever. I took the job twelve months ago as a quick fix until I found something that paid better. But this city rarely had opportunities and if they did, they filled up before anyone could think twice. A quick glance over my shoulder, and Greg was back at the till, shaking his head, counting the money again. *Asshole.* As if I'd steal the money. He probably took it and forgot.

I popped two more fries into my mouth and regretted it at once as my stomach riled up.

"Are we still up for tonight?" Cherry said, examining her long red nails nonchalantly that she obsessively wore as a tribute to her name.

My birthday. Right. It was easy to forget about things like that with how my life had been going lately. Or maybe it was how the world seemed to be going lately. Ever since *they* had taken over. Staring out at the sky again, I saw a jet fly by, a long electronic sign shooting out from behind it, reminding us all about registration, as if we could forget.

February 3, 2017 was when the world fell apart. It was done quietly. Everyone went to sleep the night before and woke up to an entirely different world. The churches had declared that they were messengers sent from God to warn us to change before the last days, but I was pretty sure the invaders were the gods themselves.

They told us they had come from a planet called Vepar and that they wished for everything to continue as before...but everything was different. The first thing to change was the required Registration. For some reason, only the women of the world were forced to register every six months. The Vepar wanted to know our names, ages, relationship status, and pregnancy history. Every woman was put on a mandatory special form of birth control that we were told was much healthier than the options we had available to us before. I would never admit it, but there were no terrible side effects with their birth control, and it was no longer a burden to take it. It was the only thing that I could say they had made better for us.

The next change was a mandatory "clean living"

mandate. All food that was processed, fried, or had any chemical in it besides healthy oils was removed as an option. No longer could I pick up a hamburger or a pizza anywhere. Instead, I could have lentils or cauliflower pasta, or something equally disgusting. Everyone was required to enter a gym for an hour a day and we were scanned as we arrived to keep track. The bastards of course didn't make anything that was mandatory free so my already thinly stretched budget was now non-existent. I had been pulling double shifts at the diner for a year now, which in my opinion should have covered my hour of exercise, but I was barely surviving.

"Ella?" said Cherry impatiently, annoyed that I wasn't paying attention to her.

"Sorry, just a little tired. Yeah, I'm still on for tonight. You only turn twenty-three once," I told her, the thin thread of exhaustion evident in my voice. She pretended not to notice and stood abruptly. "I've got to hit the gym and then start getting ready," she told me, kissing me on both cheeks like she was some kind of fancy European instead of a girl from Brooklyn. She then walked out the door without another word. As I stood, I realized she forgot to pay for her fries. *There goes my ability to eat at all this week*, I thought wryly to myself, not able to muster annoyance at my best friend due to my exhaustion.

"Your break ended five minutes ago," barked Greg as he emerged from the back. I managed to not roll my eyes as I picked up Cherry's empty fry tray and moved to throw it away. *It wasn't as if the diner was currently empty or that I hadn't taken a break all day*, I thought to myself as I stared around at the restaurant that had cleared out after Greg's fit. My mind conjured up a million different things I would say to Greg if I was a little braver and if I actually had other options for a job. I grabbed a rag and wiped down the already spotless table, my mind full of a million places I would rather be.

I WAS DRAGGING my feet by the time I finished even though we had hardly had any customers that afternoon. I didn't bother to say goodbye to Greg as I pushed out the front door and into the chilled air. October in New York was a glorious thing but all I could think about was how my heating bill was about to spike. I wondered how long I could survive a New York winter with just blankets. Maybe I could start sleeping in the gym locker rooms on particularly cold nights? My membership was practically as expensive as my one-bedroom loft.

Walking down the sidewalk, I couldn't help but notice all the advertisements featuring various Vepar. Another reason that they were considered gods? Their otherworldly attractiveness. They were built and shaped just like us, but somehow, they were more. Their skin was more perfect, their eye color was more intense, their hair color sparkled in the sun, their bodies were shaped like action heroes. Everything about them screamed that they were the pinnacle of what every human since the beginning of time had yearned to achieve. They were sexy bastards and it was unfair they got to be biologically more advanced on top of all the other ways they had us beat. An ad flashed across a screen and I got caught on the sidewalk, unable to take my eyes off the Vepar showing on the screen in the store window. He was beautiful. Even my hatred for their kind and the havoc they had thrust on my life couldn't prevent me from admitting that.

Just then a woman walked by wearing a perfume that my mother had always worn and whatever spell I was under was broken. Nothing, not even a ridiculously sexy face, could make me forget that the Vepar were responsible for the fact that I had been alone in the world for three years because of them.

So many people, in particular females, disappeared when the Vepar turned up on Earth. The aliens insisted they came in peace, as cliché as that sounded, and had never harmed anyone that we knew of. But the speculations spread that there was more to the Vepar's story, especially after our loved ones continued to vanish. Sometimes it felt like the rest of us were waiting for our number to be picked like a lottery, except this wasn't the kind of prize anyone would want to win. Lots of people insisted they were preparing us to breed with them, which I couldn't dismiss when we knew so little about their race. The majority of speculators insisted they were getting ready for a complete takeover of our planet, a takeover that would eliminate us. Wasn't that what invaders did? As far as I was concerned, I hated them and wanted zero to do with their kind. I wished they would vanish and return to their home planet, leaving us alone. Maybe if they hadn't come here, my parents would still be around, and I wouldn't be so alone.

I hurried along the sidewalk, tucking my handbag under my arm, dodging a young couple who stopped in the middle of the path to kiss. People flowed in and out of stores, chatting, laughing, many of them wearing gym gear. I squeezed in my hourly workout in the mornings because I couldn't think of anything worse than a spin class or doing weights after a long day on my feet at work.

I swung down an alley, leaving behind the hustle and bustle and bright lights of the city. Where I lived was about as opposite of the glitz and glamour of the city as you could get. As I walked, I passed trash cans and puddles that I was pretty sure were filled with urine. I went around the rear of the dilapidated Italian restaurant that filled up my apartment with annoying aromas that only served to remind me how hungry I was all the time. Shadows crowded in around me, and I pushed into a jog, always a little surprised at how much lighter and agile I felt since starting my gym workouts and starting to eat healthier. Didn't make me like the Vepar any more though. I missed my burgers and fries too much.

At the back of my rundown apartment, I grabbed an upside-down milk crate tucked near the wall and set it beneath the metal ladder just out of reach. I got up and seized the base of the fire escape ladder, then pulled it down. I made my way up, and once I reached the metal platform of the winding stairs, I kept going upward to the third floor. A cool breeze fluttered under my ponytail, cooling my neck, and bringing with it a tomato and garlic smell from across the alley, enticing a growl out of my stomach.

I avoided the front entrance since I was behind on my rental payments and the landlord lived on the ground floor. Like a hawk, he watched everyone who came and went, and I hoped to buy myself a few more days before I paid him by avoiding entering from the front.

Once I got to my window, I jiggled the wooden frame at the corner until it gave way. I then dragged the window up and climbed inside. Shutting it behind me, I locked it and switched on the light.

A studio apartment was all I needed, the bed on one end of the room, and the kitchen and a small table on the other side. The walls remained bare as I'd been on an unsuccessful hunt at flea markets since I'd moved in, looking for just the right images to hang. I toed off my shoes, kicking them aside, and walked across my cushioned rug that was one of the few things I had been able to find that I liked. It was the color of the brightest sky and always made me smile when I looked at it. A neighbor had held a sale and he sold it to me for twenty dollars. A bargain for sure.

I made my way to the fridge while unzipping my work uniform and shuffling it down my body as I walked. I tossed the uniform on the table, then reached into the fridge for the spinach and feta quiche and juice that I was rationing for dinner this week. The chef at work snuck me leftovers a few days ago after hours, saving my life this week since I wouldn't be able to afford any groceries with Greg cutting my check.

As part of the healthy living instigation, every morning, free bananas were made available by vendors on the sidewalk, all covered by the Vepar to encourage a healthy breakfast. The fruit went fast, so every morning at six a.m., I was down there, waiting for my small bag of goodies. Bananas and quiche would have to work this week.

By the time I finished my meager dinner, it was almost time for Cherry to arrive. I hurriedly jumped into the shower and got dressed for the night. I spun in front of the mirror in my black dress examining myself. The dress had spaghetti straps and cinched in at my waist. It also had a skirt that flowed in waves, falling about mid-thigh. It was my favorite dress and made me feel pretty which was a hard task with how worn down I always felt nowadays. I dried and styled my hair, a workout in itself since my long dark locks reached half-way down my back. I parted it at the side and sprayed the ends to keep the natural curl I had always liked. I was just picking up my mascara when a knock sounded at the door.

All I could hope was that it wasn't my landlord and

instead was Cherry running a few minutes early. *Please don't let it be him.*

The knock came again, and I exhaled the breath I'd been holding onto. I moved to the door, avoiding the wooden floorboards that creaked, and peered through the peep-hole.

Cherry stood there, wearing a grumpy expression, blowing a breath of air upward, flicking at the blonde strands cascading over her eyes.

I unlocked the door quickly and pulled it open.

"About time." She rolled her eyes and strolled inside wearing a red, shiny dress with the deepest neckline I had ever seen. It fell clear to her stomach. The side split on her skirt flashed her thigh with each step, showing off her black knee-high boots. She twirled on the spot. "What do you think? Found it at a new boutique store that specializes in dresses that are supposed to look just like the dresses worn by Hollywood stars."

I closed the door and turned to face my friend. "It's gorgeous. You look so sexy," I said almost wistfully, thinking that I wasn't as excited about my old dress anymore.

"Exactly what I'm going for. And you look so cute, babe. We're going to have a blast for your birthday. Pick up some guys." She winked, her attention falling to my bare feet. She furrowed her brow at the fact that I wasn't ready.

"Give me two secs and I'll be ready," I told her, rushing to the bathroom to finish applying my make-up and then quickly stepping into my black heels. We left my apartment, out the front way, after Cherry's protest on using the fire exit. And it must have been my lucky day when my landlord didn't make an appearance. Cherry called an Uber and by the time we reached the club, I'd forgotten about my crappy day. I was ready to get drunk and party.

We stepped out on to the sidewalk in front of a building that must have once been a warehouse. The brick walls had all been painted black, along with the double doors. Golden words sat over the entrance on a plaque that seemed to glow. *The Garage.*

A bouncer stood outside, decked out in black.

Cherry grabbed me by the elbow and walked me closer. "Everyone's going to this club. It's the hottest ticket in town!"

The bouncer studied us for the longest time. When he finally opened the door, I offered him a smile as I passed by, reaching into my handbag as we walked to put away the ID that he hadn't asked for. An explosion of music poured out of the establishment; a deep, fast beat that made my blood seem to pump faster.

Cherry dragged me inside, giggling and pushing aside the black curtains in the entryway. We entered the nightclub.

The music vibrated around us. The floor beneath my feet bounced with each beat, and my stomach swirled with excitement. The black theme continued inside, a circular bar with blue lights surrounding the dance floor. Overhead there was a second floor, and people were hanging by the railing, looking down at the dance floor and its mass of writhing people. Wall to wall was filled with people dancing, no room for much else. Beaming lights sailed overhead, while the DJ stood in a cage elevated over the dance floor.

"Wow. This is fantastic!" I couldn't stop grinning, and Cherry squeezed my hand at the delight in my voice.

"Told you." She drew me deeper into the crowds. Bodies squished up against me as we walked, and my feet were trampled on a couple of times. It was to be expected in a place this packed.

"We need drinks," I called out, trying to be loud enough to get past the noise, and Cherry glanced back, nodding.

By the time we reached the bar, we found a small open space to breath. "This place is sick." I glanced around, marveling again at the fact that the place was filled to the brim with what seemed like a million people. I couldn't wait to get out on the dance floor.

Cherry said something, but I didn't hear her because my gaze had settled on three men sitting at the end of the bar, one of them sizing me up. All high cheekbones, he wore a mischievous grin. Except, I'd seen him before. I wracked my brain, thinking for a few moments before it finally hit me. I'd seen him on a billboard in the streets.

I gasped and rocked on my heels, grasping Cherry's arm. Panic dug its claws into my chest. "Did you know, there're Vepar here!"

She wiggled her eyebrows. "Of course. It's a Vepar nightclub."

2

*M*y skin was crawling, and I felt sick to my stomach. I looked at my best friend who was making eyes at a Vepar a few chairs away before turning to scan the rest of the crowded room. Now that I was looking at everyone in the room it was impossible to miss the fact that they were more than just humans. Every single being in the room looked like they had marched off the cover of a high fashion spread of supernaturally gorgeous individuals. Standing among such beautiful beings in the dress that I had thought was so good-looking before, I now felt like a dowdy child that had shown up at the wrong party.

As my gaze skipped across the room, my eyes got caught on three Vepar seated at a booth a few feet away. I pushed my hair behind an ear, nervous as hell. While everyone in the room was beautiful, these three were enough to make me forget how much I hated the Vepar for half a second. While two of them were gazing around the room disinterestedly, the third was staring right at me. His hair was tousled, but not in an artificial way like was the current style. The dark blonde locks were cropped close on the sides, but longer on top, and had enough wave that I suspected they were impossible to tame. Sitting on the far side of the booth, I could see his sexy broad shoulders, emphasized by the perfect cut of his suit. He would have looked almost too perfect if it weren't for the fact that his tie was askew, as if he'd been yanking on it, and the fact that his body seemed to hum with a kind of restless energy like he was looking for something even though he was at a club. His cool blue eyes seemed to see right into my soul and coupled with the hard-as-steel jaw, he was very intimidating. Everything about him was intimidating. And sexy. Really damn sexy.

"Ella, I need twenty dollars," said Cherry, yanking my attention from the blonde predator.

"What?" I asked, my brain a little scrambled from the intense stare down I was just engaging in.

"I ordered us shots. I need to pay," she said in an annoyed voice, gesturing at the Vepar waiter who was impatiently waiting for us.

I looked at her wide-eyed. "Um sure," I said, cringing as I got a twenty out of my wallet. A twenty that I couldn't afford to part with after the debacle at the diner today. She had at least the decency to offer me an apologetic shrug as she grabbed the money.

"I guess I forgot my wallet at home," she said, handing the money to the bartender who then pushed what looked like four candy apple green shots towards us. Alcohol had managed to stay available despite the health restrictions. Apparently the Vepar were just as fond of drinks as us humans were.

I tried to push away my annoyance at the fact that I was paying for my own birthday shots by draining my two shots as quickly as I could. If I was going to get through this night, it was going to be because I was drunk. As I gasped at the burn, I could immediately feel myself relaxing. My muscles unflexed, and my breath slowed down.

"Those were just regular shots, right?" I asked, as the room began to spin a little bit.

"It's a Vepar bar," she said to me haughtily. "Of course, I was going to have us try Vepar liquor."

She slid off her barstool ungracefully, her almost non-existent dress briefly flashing the fact that she wasn't wearing underwear, and I hurriedly averted my eyes as she nonchalantly adjusted herself.

"I think it's time to see if the Vepar men like me as much as human men do," she said, tossing her long blonde hair behind her and doing a shimmy. She scanned the room before homing in on a target, a well-dressed Vepar with slicked black hair who was making eyes in our direction. I couldn't be sure, but it looked like he was looking at me rather than Cherry.

Unperturbed, Cherry grabbed my arm and began to drag me behind her, completely forgetting that this was my birthday and I might have something else that I wanted to do besides be her wingman for the night. Cherry was already getting sloppy from the shots we'd taken at the bar and she narrowly missed running into a waiter who was hustling by with a full tray of glasses. Unfortunately, her narrowly missing the waiter meant that I couldn't swerve out of the way in time and the tray knocked me in the head, sending me falling backwards, the back of my knees hitting something hard. I stumbled into what felt like a rock-solid seat that I realized belatedly was someone's lap.

My cheeks burned from falling into someone, and I sat frozen. I looked up into a shocking green gaze that I immediately recognized as belonging to one of the men that I had noticed earlier, and then I immediately averted my eyes.

That wasn't much better as I could see that the Vepar all around me were staring at me, the clumsy human.

I shook my head, telling myself to turn my head and face the situation. Turning, my breath caught a little. He was a damn good-looking man...alien...Vepar...whatever they were called. I could fall into his gaze, and I suddenly found myself picturing us naked with me beneath him. I trembled at the thought, yet I couldn't get his face out of my thoughts. So gorgeous it would stop anyone in their tracks. I'm sure he was used to that kind of attention, based on the little smirk on his face. I'm sure females of both species froze when they crossed his path. He had the greenest eyes I had ever seen. They had a haunting twinkle to them that just added to his allure. He looked like he could see all of my inappropriate thoughts. Heat crawled up my neck, and I prayed that wasn't the case.

Looking around for help, I caught a glance of Cherry walking out the door with what had to be one of the only other human males in the club. Tears gathered in my eyes and my throat thickened at the fact that my so-called best friend was leaving me on my birthday in a Vepar club of all places. And we'd just arrived too. I squirmed to get up, but the arm around my waist held firm.

"What's the hurry, my pet?" he whispered in my ear, his breath sending tremors down my spine.

"I saw someone I know. I should go say hello," I responded weakly, not wanting to let him know that I was now all alone at the club.

"I can hear your heartbeat, pet. I know you are lying." His words carried a light growl, and while they should have scared me, I found myself becoming intrigued. I twisted around, still trapped in his lap, and tumbled into those stunning eyes again that were too pretty to be human. They reaffirmed I wasn't sitting in the lap of a human.

He was most definitely a Vepar.

My breath hitched all the way down to my lungs, and as if sensing my fear, he smiled. His upper lip lifted slightly, a dimple crinkling on his chin. Warmth radiated from his expression, and his gaze fixed on me as if a secret lay between us. Then he gave me a knowing nod.

The blush burning my cheeks was a dead giveaway of the way he affected me. My mouth twitched, and I fought a smile, reminding myself whose lap I sat in.

The monsters who came onto Earth and took over. The ones that were most likely responsible for all the missing people, missing people like my parents.

I'd heard people say to stay hidden when a Vepar made an appearance. *If they don't know you exist, they can't take you.*

And I'd ruined that royally by landing in one's lap. Frantically I looked around again to see if there was any way out of the situation. I needed to run, get away as fast as I could. I needed to forget tonight, forget Cherry, forget my birthday.

I wriggled in his grasp. "You can let me go now."

"What's the rush?" he said, his voice velvety smooth against my ear, and the shivers returned to my skin from his breath on my neck. If my body reacted that quickly from his closeness, I had no hope of saying no to him. He'd somehow get me in bed with him, and before long, I'd vanish from society and probably end up in a prison on another planet. Or so the rumors insisted.

I glanced down at his strong arms, the corded muscles beneath the tanned skin. His shirt was the color of midnight and was rolled to his elbows, giving him a casual look despite the fanciness of the club. Around us a mix of Vepar and human women danced, cheered, and drank. I didn't see any sign of the Vepar's two companions that I had seen him with earlier. Had they separated so they could study the humans and select their prey?

I twisted in his lap to look at him again, and it was a terrible mistake. My heart skipped a beat and I lost my words being this close to someone so incredibly handsome. My fingers tingled with the urgency to reach over and touch his face to see if he was real.

Was this his real form? Was it possible for a whole planet to be full of nothing but genetic perfection? if so, it must have been disappointing to arrive on Earth to find we weren't all spectacular models. I lowered my gaze, curling my shoulders forward, reminding myself I was nothing spectacular. My work uniform hung over my thin frame during the day, and my black dress tonight was nothing special. I wore my dark chestnut hair in a ponytail most days, though I had toyed with the idea of putting purple highlights in it. But just like with most things, I never gained the courage.

I pushed myself out of his grasp, suddenly feeling less scared, but more out of place. I didn't belong here, not with these gorgeous people, not at his club, and definitely not pretending this man would be interested in me. Even as an extraterrestrial being, he'd overlook a simple female like me, unless his goal was to hunt down a slave. Even Cherry had picked up a guy, while every inch of me itched to run back to my apartment.

Quickly, I climbed out of his lap, suddenly appreciating his kindness in showing me interest. I shyly glanced away and turned toward the exit when iron fingers wrapped around my wrist.

"Where are you going, my pet?"

I twisted around to face the man with the devilish eyes,

his strong hand wrapped around mine like a shackle.

"I made a mistake in coming here," I answered, not sure if I was talking about coming here without knowing it was a Vepar club or coming here in the first place because I didn't belong. Something about the tenderness in his gaze coaxed me to speak the truth, because I suspected he picked up on small nuances like my nervousness, that I was alone, and how vulnerable I appeared.

I might be vulnerable, but I wasn't about to forget how dangerous the creature was holding on to me.

"Humans have a saying that there's no such thing as coincidences. Do you believe that?" he said randomly, tracing my lips with a whisper soft touch. Somehow the act seemed more intimate than sex. This being was looking at me like he knew all of my secrets or at least felt that my secrets belonged to him. He's touching me so possessively, not even pausing for a moment to ask my permission. I'm suddenly even more aware that the creature in front of me is a predator hidden behind a pretty face. I have to leave.

I shrugged, trying to hide the fact that I felt almost debilitated by fear, and tucked a strand of hair behind an ear nonchalantly. "Haven't given it much thought. Guess if enough strange things keep happening, I'd question the coincidence."

His thumb on the hand that was holding my arm in a vice grip started to rub a circle on the inside of my wrist as he held my gaze, so intent and focused I had no choice but to start shivering. Tremors wiggled south to the pit of my stomach and lower. I'd never had a man stare at me with such depth, not even the boys who'd shown semi-interest in me in the past. This here...this was something else.

"What can I get you to drink?" he asked smoothly, his eyes still on me like I was a shot of single malt whiskey.

The voices, thumping music, and mass crowd in the club floated somewhere behind me. My eyes flitted anywhere besides his face as my mind raced with how to escape. As much as my body responded to his attentiveness, how the heat between my thighs inflamed into an inferno, I was sure I wouldn't survive the night if I stayed any longer.

"Thanks, but maybe next time." I said, trying to draw my hand from his without success.

"Sometimes the hardest thing in life is letting go," he said randomly, finally letting go of my hand.

I should have turned and run at that moment, but something in the way he said that last statement made me hesitate. "What do you mean?"

"Change is never easy."

I blinked against the lights flashing in our direction. "I don't know what you're talking about," I said, the panic starting to bleed into my voice. I regretted my outburst at once as a glimmer of amusement arose in his eyes at my blatant fear.

"You'll find out soon, pet." He released my hand, and I stumbled on the spot. "You better go catch up to your friend."

His riddles made no sense, but considering he knew I came with Cherry meant he'd been watching me before I fell into his lap. I spun and pushed through the crowds, needing to leave, get away, and never visit this club again.

"I'll be seeing you around," he called out, and I glanced over my shoulder one more time. But the seat he lounged in was empty.

Where the hell was he?

I ran from the club like I was being chased by demons, the feeling that someone was watching me settling over my skin like dread.

3

---

*T*he next morning everything seemed like it was just a bad dream. Especially when Cherry banged on the door at 7am, immediately beginning to bitch and complain about what a "crappy lay" that guy from the bar was. Of course, she didn't apologize for ditching me at a bar full of creatures she knew I was terrified of. It was the Cherry show as usual. And like usual, I listened to everything she had to say while I got ready for work.

Cherry's father was some bigwig on Wall Street and still provided for his "little girl." Even though his little girl was now 25 and has never worked a day in her life. Cherry always said that her job was to find a rich husband because she was born to be a socialite. It hadn't happened yet for her, but she certainly gave it her best effort.

"Are you even listening to me?" she blurted, while helping herself to the last of my cereal and milk. I guessed the free bananas at the Vepar stand out on the sidewalk would have to do for breakfast.

"You're going to have to eat that as we leave," I explained somewhat impatiently. "I have to get to work."

"Can't you take one day off? We were out so late last night, I'm wrecked." I didn't bother mentioning that she had no idea how late I was out until since she ditched me.

"Sorry, after what happened yesterday with my pay being docked, I can't miss a shift," I told her, beginning to push her out the door. Something I couldn't identify flickered in her eyes but it quickly disappeared. It almost looked like guilt.

Not having the energy or time to analyze Cherry this morning, I finish pushing her out the door, then locked the door behind us. I learned the hard way after I came home one night and my loft was completely wrecked that I could not leave Cherry unattended at my place. I wasn't sure why she came to my place so often in the first place since her father paid for a luxurious apartment by Central Park. There was a lot I didn't understand about that girl.

Cherry and I had just parted ways, and I was about to cross the street to arrive at the diner when a luxurious black town car pulled up in front of me. The back-seat window rolled down slowly. I rubbed the goosebumps out of my arms. A beautiful blue-eyed man with hair so blonde it seemed to sparkle in the sunlight that streamed through the car window was staring at me from inside the car. It was the Vepar that had been watching me last night before I fell in his green-eyed companion's lap.

"Need a ride, Ella?" he asked, his smooth voice sending shivers down my spine.

He knew my name? I tried to remember if I had told his Vepar friend my name last night, but I couldn't remember. My mind felt addled, everything from the night before seemed blurry, like it had all been in my imagination. A terrible dream that had me waking up feeling hot and uncomfortably turned on this morning...

Shaking my head at the direction my thoughts had turned, I turned my attention back to the fact that a Vepar that I had never met was offering me a ride and somehow knew my name. There was no way that this was a coincidence and he had just happened to be driving by and decided to offer me a ride after his friend told him about me. Yeah, right.

Everyone said to stay away from the Vepar, but it appeared I'd gained the attention of multiple ones last night. I'd have to correct that now.

"Thanks, but I'm just going down the block," I told him, my voice trembling as I started to jog away as the crosswalk light turned green, giving me the okay to cross the street. The truth was the diner was quite a bit more than a block away, but I would run twice that distance if it kept me away from the charmingly dangerous stranger. What did he want?

I didn't turn around to see if he was still there as I ran away. It wasn't necessary since I could feel his gaze following me until I made it around the block and was out of sight.

Once I arrived at work, I stored my bag in the locker in the back and put on my apron, then I hurried into the unusually full diner and started my shift. The place was packed. Where had everyone come from today?

The business meant that the day flew by fast. As usual, Sandy had called in sick, so I served all the customers on my own. It was amazing that Sandy could consistently fail to come into work, yet she managed to keep her job. I wondered if her new boyfriend was actually Greg.

Speaking of Greg, he didn't say a word to me all day, not even hello, but he watched me like a hawk, especially each time I used the register for customer payments. Bastard still believed I stole the money the other day, and that annoyed me more than I cared to admit. I knew I shouldn't care what he thought but I worked my ass off, and he was treating me like a criminal. With each passing hour, the walls of the diner seemed to close in around me as my exhaustion and frustration grew. I kept going, in auto mode, taking orders, smiling, delivering food, and cleaning tables. Luckily little thought was needed for those activities because my mind was far too occupied with all of my current problems plus the new Vepar one. Questions like, how was I ever going to get ahead in life? Was I ever going to have enough money to do more than just scrape by?

I finally admitted to myself that I needed to get back to the job hunt. There had to be something, even another waitress job that would pay better and that wouldn't work me to the bone. Not that I had an aversion to working hard, but I needed at least a little bit better quality of life if I was going to live to see my next birthday.

At the end of my shift, I stepped out of the diner with my handbag, pretending not to hear Greg complain to the cook about having to close for the night on his own, and how he needed more reliable staff. Unlike other days, I didn't jump and take the responsibility. If he didn't trust me, then why should I work after hours for almost nothing in return?

Outside, orange and blues streaked across the afternoon sky and a cool breeze cooled the perspiration on my neck. My heels ached with each step from being on my feet all day, but something about the colors overhead reminded me of my parents. A longing swept through my chest at not having them in my life, not having someone to talk to when I felt so alone. We grew up in an apartment, and like me, they lived from one paycheck to the next, but we were happy, and we had each other.

Instead of crossing Bexter Road to head home, I kept strolling straight ahead past storefronts and people shopping, unable to stop remembering my parents. And when I missed them, one location always eased the sorrow somewhat. A little slice of paradise where I could leave society behind and I could think in peace.

It wasn't long before I stood in front of the six-foot-tall gates made of twisted metal rods. The ends were curled in a circular pattern, and while spiders had made the corners of the gate their home with a maze of webs, it still was a beautiful sight to me. Behind me lay the city museum, but it was closed as it was past 4pm, which meant that most of the patrons to the garden had left as well. I had one hour to enjoy Greenwood Botanical Garden before it closed.

The crunch of tires sounded behind me before I could go in, and I turned around, for some reason expecting the black sedan from this morning to be waiting for me. Instead a white hatchback full of laughing teenagers coasted past. I laughed at my jumpiness and proceeded into the garden.

The incident turned my attention from my parents back to the Vepar. He had offered me a ride this morning. Just thinking about it made my earlier goosebumps return. I wanted to believe that it had just been chance that he had found me as he had been passing by. But I knew I was in denial.

I had been unextraordinary my entire life. The most out of the ordinary thing that had ever happened to me was becoming an orphan. Human men didn't pay me any attention. Why would a Vepar?

I hurried into the gardens, tiny pebbles crunching under my worn-out sneakers. I silently chanted to myself that everything would be okay...it had to be.

Lofty trees with bottle green leaves flanked my path, and the blossoming landscape was filled with the fragrance of jasmine. Up ahead, copious flowery beds lay in every direction, segmented by colors. Whites, fuschias, oranges, and violets. I followed the curved path to where the trees grew denser and shadows fell over the land. Birds chirped and the scratching of dried leaves indicated that little critters or lizards were scurrying through the foliage beside me.

There wasn't a person in sight, which on my most days I preferred. Today the solitude made the hairs on my arms stand on end. I kept glancing over my shoulder, feeling like someone was watching me. But every time I turned to look, there was no one there. So, I kept walking.

I marched up the hill. I passed the glass greenhouse before crowning the hill which gave the best view of the city. From this height, the city seemed to lay beneath my feet. You could see the way the tall buildings had been so carefully regimented and ordered. The descending sun illuminated the shimmering glow of pollution that lay just above the city.

Up here I could escape it. Getting my fill of the view, I took a seat on a bench overlooking a Koi fish pond several feet away. From here, the water looked opaque green, its surface ruffling from the breeze. There were lily pads in bloom, and I watched as their white petals fluttered in the wind.

I inhaled deeply and slowly savoring the smell of the greenery around me.

Dad had once said that when he died, he wanted his soul bound to the gardens so he could roam our favorite place forever. Maybe it was wishful thinking on my part, but I came here often in the hope that if I didn't sense his spirit, he was somewhere out there still alive.

This had been our place. My parents would bring me to this park for family picnics every week. But that had been before the world changed, before the Vepar took over...before I lost everything.

With a long exhale, I dropped my handbag near my feet and remembered the tales of how he'd proposed to Mom. He had brought her to this very location with takeout burgers from their favorite burger place for them to eat, and a diamond ring in his pocket. He had used his last savings to buy the band, but that was my Dad. He always told me he'd sell the clothes off his back for my mom. He would have done anything for her...anything for us. They had loved each other with a love that everyone around them had envied.

Mom had admitted to me once after Dad had told that story for the thousandth time that she knew what he had planned all along. But when he fell to his knees in this exact spot, she had still burst out crying from joy even though she expected it.

Something in my chest tightened as I pictured the scene, and then of course my mind inevitably tried to picture my own engagement. Somewhere in the far-off future...if at all. Tears pricked my eyes thinking about the fact that my parents wouldn't be there to see it, or even hear about it.

Heaviness sat in my chest, tearing me apart at not knowing if my parents were still alive. For so long, I told myself they were somewhere, maybe held captive, but it had been years since they vanished. Not a word or note...not anything. They wouldn't have just left me.

Hope.

I held onto it like a lifeline, praying one day I'd see them again, see their smiles, hear their voices. I sighed. I was just kidding myself.

The minutes ticked by as I sat in the park, my mind heavy with sorrow. The shadows surrounding me stretched

across the landscape, and the fiery sky darkened. A quick
check of my cell showed I only had ten minutes remaining
before closing time. My stomach was growling in hunger
too, so I collected my bag and headed home.

Outside the gardens, cars filled the road. As I turned
down the sidewalk, a black vehicle parked across the road
caught my attention. It was the same one from this morning,
the same one I had been looking for over my shoulder all
day. It sat there with its tinted windows rolled up, and my
stomach sunk all the way to my toes.

Please don't let it be him. There were a million black
sedans in this city. I told myself it could be anyone. Tucking
my chin into my chest, I held my bag tight under my armpit,
and walked as quickly as I could away.

Looking back, the car was still parked, and I memorized
the number plate. VRA001. When the brake lights came on,
a small cry fell from my lips.

I started running, my heart hitting the back of my throat
as my unreasonable fear grew. The park stretched out for
blocks, so when the cars stopped at the traffic lights, I
crossed the road toward the store fronts and apartment
buildings. Without pausing, I sprinted as fast as I could,
dodging an elderly couple waiting for the bus, and swishing
past a group of girls chatting. One quick look back showed
me that the black car was driving off in the opposite
direction.

I should have breathed easy as its tail lights faded into
the distance, but I couldn't stop running and I couldn't
remove the fear clinging to my ribs. A sudden gust of wind
came out of nowhere, ripping at my hair and clothes,
tossing garbage from an overturned trash can across the
ground. But still I kept running.

By the time I arrived home, I could barely catch my

breath. I didn't bother going around to the back of the building to go up the fire escape. Instead, I ran through the front, not even looking at my landlord who was skulking around the lobby. Once I got to my apartment, I shut the door behind me fast, and then I ran across the apartment and locked the window too.

Once finished securing the place with the meager security my place offered me, I flopped onto the couch in the dimly lit main room, still clutching my bag, and trying to catch my breath.

"Shit!" I started laughing somewhat hysterically at the thought that I had just run across town for no other reason than I had seen one of the million black sedans in the city. I was being ridiculous.

A small voice inside my head reminded me that there *was* a chance it had been him. The notion sat like a boulder in my gut. I had heard the warnings about the Vepars since they had arrived, people saying that you should never gain the attention of the beautiful ones, what if I had?

I sat my bag on the cushion next to me when my phone dinged with a message. I flinched and dug my hand into the bag to grab the phone. Greg. My boss never messaged me, and I frowned, reading the message.

I've changed your shift from day to afternoon. This includes closing up the diner. Starts immediately.

Bastard! Reading the message over and over didn't change the cold hard facts. He was cutting back my hours and wanted me to clean and close up while he left early. He was pissed because I hadn't volunteered my free time, and now I was paying the price with a permanent punishment if I didn't find another job quick. My chest burned up, feeling as if it might detonate like a supernova.

Who the hell did he think he was?

I tossed my phone onto the couch and leaned forward, hugging my middle. Fewer hours meant less money, so this made my decision to find a new job even easier. First thing in the morning, I'd visit every food joint in the city with my resume.

I glanced across the room at the fridge, thinking about the stale quiche that awaited me for dinner. My eyes raked across my gym bag as I looked around the room. I groaned and sagged into my seat.

"Oh, crap!" I'd forgotten to do my daily gym time, and I didn't need another reason for a Vepar to pay me attention. I dragged myself off the couch and headed to the closet to change into lycra pants and a tank top, hating my life while mapping out the shortest route to the gym that would keep me from prying eyes...or black sedans.

4

The morning winds were ferocious, pulling at the nicer clothes I had put on to apply for jobs. The plastic folder with copies of my resume trembled in my hand from the breeze, threatening to fly away if I didn't hold on tightly. Cars honked as they fought through traffic on their morning commute down the two-lane road. I pressed past the ocean of pedestrians on the sidewalk and made my way toward the Good Morning Café located on the corner of a busy intersection. Once inside the establishment, I pushed the door against the whistling wind. Finally closed, I patted down my hair and straightened my posture before glancing at the half empty diner and catching the eye of a young man in jeans and a freshly pressed white shirt. He studied me with amusement on his face and what seemed like interest. The badge on his chest said his name was Jack.

Then he strode closer. "Hi, there. Seat for one?" he asked with a fake smile I knew too well.

"I'd like to speak to your manager, please."

He shook his head. "Not in, sorry. Can I help you?"

Chewing on my lower lip, I pulled out my one-page resume from the plastic folder and handed it to him. "I'm wondering if you were hiring?"

I handed him my resume, but he didn't take it. "I have several years' experience in waitressing, ordering supplies, and even stepping in as the cook." I said quickly. My voice sounded nervous even to me, and heat crawled up my neck at the thought of another rejection.

"Look," he began, and already my gut clenched. I'd heard the tone he used at the last five diners I visited, and I knew what came next. An excuse of them not hiring at the moment, the place was downsizing, or I wasn't the right fit... whatever that meant.

I lowered my unaccepted resume and turned to leave. I stopped mid-turn when Jack surprised me by saying, "The manager will be in in about a half an hour, so how about you give him your resume then?"

I glanced up at his kind smile and grinned, my mouth tugging into a smile at the first positive response I had received today. "Thank you."

"Follow me." He waved me into the café, and I saw the spark of recognition in his eyes, the understanding of how hard it was to find a job. "I'll get you a coffee on the house until he arrives."

I was already in love with this place, not to mention, having someone treat me like a human and with respect.

The aroma of coffee filled the air, immediately making me feel a bit better. A shiny orange color adorned the corners of the small round tables and the napkins were the same hue. Everything else had a rustic wooden look that seemed like it would make a customer feel right at home. Light jazz music played from the speakers, and customers chatted over their breakfast and coffee. I loved it here. The door opened behind me as someone else walked in, bringing with it a cold breeze. I shivered slightly.

Jack pulled out a chair at a small table near the window, overlooking the hustle and bustle outside. "Won't be long," he said with a gentle smile.

I took a seat, and Jack went to attend to a customer waving him down.

It was about thirty minutes before the bell on the door rang again, signaling that someone had just walked in. Looking up, I expected to see a stranger strolling through the door. Instead I saw *Him*. It was the green-eyed god from the night at the club. The one whose compelling voice had made me want to curl up in his arms forever. The one who called me his "pet."

He wore tailed black pants, and a blue, long-sleeved shirt, looking like he belonged in a boardroom. Except, I'd never seen a man look this good in business attire. I suspected he wore only the best brands considering how perfectly the clothes flowed over his strong form, emphasizing the broadness of his chest and shoulders...the way his waist tapered in. I lifted my gaze before he caught me staring.

What was he doing here, anyway?

He strolled into the café as if he had been here a million times before, except he wasn't looking for the host so he could be sat at a table, he was looking right at me. Almost as if he knew I'd be here.

I was standing up from the table as he sat down across from me.

"Sit down, pet," he told me with a grin. I immediately sat, almost as if I couldn't help but bend to the authority in his voice. That intangible quality that threaded around his words made me want to listen to everything he had to say.

A couple tables down, Jack sent me an inquisitive glance. I averted my gaze so he wouldn't feel like he needed to come over to my rescue.

"Why are you following me?" I finally asked after we had sat there just staring at each other for what seemed like ten minutes.

"Who said I was following you?" he replied with a grin. "Maybe I just felt like an omelet from this charming establishment."

"Look, I'm not interesting, I promise. There are a million other girls who I'm sure would amuse you much more than me. Please, just leave me alone. And tell your friend that he needs to stop following me as well," I added as an afterthought, thinking about the black car. I assumed that they had to be friends of some sort since they had been talking at the club.

"How do you know what I'm looking for?" he asked.

I just stared at him, moving my lips dumbly but not knowing what to say.

"Ella, let me be perfectly clear that you *are* what I'm looking for. And that's not going to change."

Every inch of me froze over. "How do you know my name?"

He glanced down at my resume sitting face up on the table. My name was on full display, along with my address. *Fuck.*

I snatched the file and tucked it under my arm, then finally stood to leave. Even a new job wasn't worth staying here with this creature.

"Where are you going?" he mused, with that grin that both filled me with dread and made my stomach hurt with how attractive it was at the same time. "There's nowhere you can go that we won't find you," he said. And somehow, I knew he spoke the truth. But to hear the words out loud left me shaking. I curled in on myself at the realization that I was trapped.

Stupid, stupid, stupid. Why hadn't I run away that night the second I had realized what he was?

He stood before I could leave. "Stay, enjoy breakfast on me," he said, throwing a few bills on the table that looked like they would cover a dozen meals at this place. "And if you get the job, just know you'll be calling in to give your notice, very, very soon." He stared at me with such intent that I didn't doubt his words, even if they didn't sound menacing. The threat behind them lingered in my mind. Was that how my parents went missing? Vepar decided to target them, and then one day, poof, they simply disappeared? My knees weakened at the thought of that happening to me.

On that ominous note he walked by me, making sure to brush up against my body as he did so. Hard and solid, he smelled of fresh air and a sexy musk. A thought I cursed myself for. I was an idiot for thinking of him as attractive in any way. Especially considering he'd clearly just threatened me. I knew better than most that beauty was only skin deep.

What could I even do? The authorities had all been infiltrated by the Vepar, and what they said went.

I slid shakily back down in my seat once I heard the bell ring on the door signaling he had left. My hands curled in my lap, and I stared outside the window to see him strolling across the road before vanishing into a crowd of people.

What was I going to do? I couldn't stay here. I had to leave, but where would I go with no money? I stared at the notes of $100 on the table more carefully now, noting he'd dropped $500 without a care. I barely came close to making that much in weeks of working lately.

At that moment, Jack came back. "The owner just got here if you still want to talk to him," he said, giving me a concerned look. "Is everything okay?"

I nodded numbly. In another life maybe I could work here, maybe I would even have ended up dating Jack, he was attractive and seemed sweet enough. And he certainly was giving me the look like he was interested. But I couldn't even picture what having a normal life would be like now. My head hurt and fear crowded in my mind like the cobwebs on the front gates of the botanical garden.

I was about to leave without talking to the owner, but a kind looking man in his 60s with salt and pepper streaked hair chose that moment to show up at my table.

"This is the owner, Mr. Kinsley." Jack said as he gestured to the man.

Mr. Kinsley gave me a kind smile that didn't hold any of the menace or sleaziness that my boss, Greg's did.

Within twenty minutes, he'd offered me the job and I was set to start the next day. I bounced on the inside, wanting to scream with excitement. Slipping the money off the table that the Vepar had left for me, I waved goodbye to Jack and Mr. Kinsley, and I walked out of the cafe in a daze. Had that just happened?

I should have been more excited, especially knowing I could now march over and tell Greg to fuck himself. But I couldn't find it in me to fully celebrate. Not after the conversation with the annoyingly attractive Vepar hanging over my head. I still didn't even know his name. Yet he seemed to know everything about me including where I was going to be in a random job search. And now he knew my address. Hell!

Sighing, I found myself heading back to the Botanical Gardens, needing the comfort that only they could provide. As I strolled through the blossoming paths, my mind seemed to clear. Surely this was a short-term fascination for the Vepar. There was no way someone like me could hold his attention. Everything would be fine, it had to be. I was a nobody in a city filled with attractive women.

I had almost talked myself off the ledge when I rounded a corner, and there sitting on a park bench, reading a book, was the third Vepar that had been watching me that night at the club. While the other two had overwhelming beauty, this Vepar's was more understated. With thick hair the color of mahogany, and eyes that reminded me of caramel, he studied me as if I was the most interesting thing that he'd ever seen. He tilted his head to the side, and I could tell instantly he enjoyed observing, studying, analyzing things. Most likely people. In this case... Me.

We both exchanged looks, and the pause should have been awkward, but it wasn't. "So, are you following me then as well?" I finally asked, breaking the tranquility, praying and wishing on everything that he wasn't here for me and this place could remain a safe space for me.

He cocked his head, still studying me. I might as well be an insect under a microscope. He seemed like he was trying to see everything about me in that moment. My past, my fear, my loneliness.

"Well, do you actually speak?" I asked, not even recognizing my bravery...or the stupidity I displayed.

At my comment, he smiled, and it was the most devilish grin I'd ever seen. "I like your directness," he said. His eyes lit up, and the corners of his mouth creased into an even wider smile. His smile was somehow so much more though because he smiled with more than his mouth. I could hear it in his voice. I took back whatever I'd been thinking before about his beauty being more understated than the other two. He was glorious. A thought I immediately wanted to punch myself for.

"Did you know that there are around 391,000 different types of plant species that your scientists have discovered on this planet so far?" he asked in a smooth, cultured voice.

I stared at him like he was crazy.

"Um, okay. That didn't really answer my question," I said, beginning to back away slowly, thinking that this Vepar was perhaps a little unhinged.

He grinned bashfully, if a ridiculously good looking Vepar could really be bashful. "Sorry, I've been trying to think of the perfect thing to say to you when I got to talk to you. And obviously that wasn't it."

He patted the empty bench next to him, looking at me expectantly. I should have turned and ran, but then what? Keep bumping into these three Vepar who seemed to be paying me way too much attention? The Vepar in the cafe had warned me to not get comfortable with a new job, so I'd be a fool to ignore this threat and not discover more about their intentions. This creature seemed kinder than the others, almost human with his attempt at finding something interesting to say to me. Thinking it over, I finally took several slow steps forward and joined him on the bench, placing my bag between us as a makeshift barrier.

"Why are you here?" I asked, glancing up at him as he reclined, his arms by his side, his gaze drifting off into the distance toward the city. The morning sun illuminated the golden stubble across his strong jawline, lighter than the hair on top of his head. The corded muscles in his neck lured me in. He was the perfect package just like the others.

Many people had said their beauty came from an illusion they used, a disguise to conceal their real appearance. And if that were true, what did they look like underneath? Scaly with a tail? I laughed internally at myself because I'd obviously watched too many science fiction movies. Where would he even hide his tail?

Never in a million years would I have pictured myself near someone as handsome as him, but then again, who would have guessed Earth would end up invaded by aliens. I almost laughed out loud that time at how ridiculous it sounded, but here I was sitting by a real live alien.

"Did you know there's a Russian village, Oymyakon, which experienced the lowest recorded temperature for a location permanently inhabited by people. -96 degrees."

I met his gaze, unable to understand why he was talking about that. "Why do you do that?"

"Do what?" he shrugged nonchalantly.

"Keep ignoring my question."

"Perhaps you're not listening close enough to see I *am* answering your question."

I ran a hand down my face, frustration bubbling in my chest as I recalled the other Vepars' riddled way of talking to me in the club. But these men weren't from our world, so maybe this was their way of communicating. Never directly but hinting at things. So, I'd try to remain patient and follow their logic.

"Okay." I twisted to face him, tucking a bent leg between us. "So, your world is frozen and is no longer inhabitable, and that's why you're here?"

He shook his head. "Look beyond the obvious answer."

I sighed heavily. "Can't you just tell me?"

But he sat there, silence filling the space between us, and he studied me, waiting for my response. Was this part of his experiment? See how the humans' mind worked, what we focused on?

"You asked why I'm here, which could be taken as either why we came to Earth or why I'm in this garden. I answered in a way that best suited both of those questions."

I blinked hard, my head buzzing with trying to make sense of his response. All right, I could do this. "This Russian village has people permanently living there despite the hellish cold, so they've learned to find a life in extreme weather. They've adapted." I met his smiling gaze. "And you're on our planet to acclimate and identify the differences. And for the garden, you want to find out more about me. To adapt." My mouth split into a grin, and I couldn't help it, especially when he nodded and smirked.

"Good girl."

That small gesture made me perversely happy as if I were back at school and I'd just passed the hardest exam. But now half a dozen more questions prodded my mind, and if getting the answer to them required this much work, I'd die of exhaustion.

"Let's start with something simple. What's your name?" I tucked loose strands of hair behind an ear.

"Why do you do *that*?" he asked, studying my hand as I lowered it from my hair.

In all honesty, I hadn't given it much thought or even noticed the habit half the time. "Nerves I guess, and-" But I paused, reminding myself who I spoke with and that this wasn't a casual conversation with a guy I crushed on. This Vepar acted normal and interested and polite, but I still had no clue about his intention. Sure, he wanted to get to know me, but why?

I cleared my throat and straightened my posture before lowering my leg and turning to face the city in the far distance. "Why are you and the other two following me? And be straight with me."

Instead of responding, he stood. "I'd better be leaving. I'll see you soon, Ella." And with those few words, he strolled down the path, leaving me alone with renewed fear bottled in my chest threatening to swallow me whole.

5

I'd had enough. No matter where I went, *they* were there. The black car with the annoyingly attractive blonde Vepar was waiting for me outside of my loft apartment every morning as I left as well as waiting at a host of other places. He never tried to talk to me again, but I could feel his gaze following me as I walked from behind those tinted windows. The black-haired, blue eyed devil was always popping up to eat at the cafe I was now working at or showing up at the gym when I was working out, or basically anywhere else I happened to find myself. I couldn't go to the botanical gardens anymore because without fail the brown haired Vepar would be there ready with more riddles for me. None of them ever answered my questions about their true intentions. They haunted my days and my nights as my dreams were filled with dark specters that followed my every move and refused to let me go. My dreams would always end with my parents' screams, begging me to help them.

Exhaustion rattled through me, like I was one of those

zombies from those movies that I hated but Cherry always insisted on watching.

I couldn't take it anymore. Three weeks followed by stalkers had left me with no choice.

I had to get away.

I couldn't function like this anymore, or I'd go crazy. I needed a second to myself so I could sort out my thoughts on what to do next.

That night I packed up a small bag filled with a few clothes as well as the money that the blue-eyed Vepar had left at the cafe along with the little bits I had been able to save the last few weeks at the busy cafe.

For a moment, I let myself feel the tinge of regret that came from leaving the first job I had ever liked. Just in these few weeks I'd already made friends and more money than I had in a few months of working at the diner. Jack and Mr. Kinley had fast become some of my favorite people who I'd ever met, and I would miss talking to them. Hopefully they didn't worry too much about me when I abruptly disappeared. Jack knew something had been going on by the way I ignored the Vepar who came into the cafe every day, going so far as to switch sections when he was sat at my tables.

Opening the window to the fire escape, I steeled myself for what lay ahead. Creeping down the stairs I kept my eyes out for any of them to appear. They seemed to know all of my habits down to what I ate every day and what I wore. It was reasonable to believe that they probably knew I used the fire escape most days because of my landlord. All I could hope was that me leaving in the middle of the night wouldn't be anticipated by them and they wouldn't be around.

I got to the ground without incident. Peering around the corner I looked at the street to see if anyone was around. I gasped when I spied the sleek, black town car, waiting across the street. Did he sleep in the car? Fear sliced across my consciousness as the full reality of the situation struck me.

This was beyond liking someone, this was an obsession.

I backed away from the street, convinced he couldn't have seen me peeking around the building, and I headed down another route. I was going to try Cherry's first. Cherry had been "busy" since my birthday with the guy she had met at the Vepar club. And like usual when she met a new guy, I hadn't seen or heard from her since then.

But she was my best friend. She would take a break from her little love bubble to help me out. She had to.

It took me twice as long to get to her apartment as usual since I had to take the long way, but I was thrilled when I managed to make it to her place without being stopped. About halfway through my trip it had started raining, but as I stood outside Cherry's place, I didn't care that I looked like a drowned rat, I was just happy that I was going to be safe.

I knocked on the door. Music played from inside along with the sound of people laughing. Was she having a party? A party that she didn't invite me to? Hurt filled my stomach, but I continued to knock on the door. *Answer, Answer, Answer*, I chanted in my head as the minutes passed and no one answered. I had no intention of returning home tonight so this had to work. What I craved more than anything was to feel safe for a little while, to laugh with my friend, and have her tell me things would be okay.

Finally, I just tried the door, and to my surprise it was unlocked. Cherry had always been lax about her security even though every human understood to lock their door since the Vepar invasion. You never knew who might be waiting outside and wanting to get in...

I walked into the entryway of her apartment where she had framed photos of the night sky; one pebbled with stars, another of the Milky Way. So many gorgeous images that didn't really fit with Cherry's style. Cherry had no clue about the constellations, nor was she even interested in anything universe related. She had once told me the pieces were conversation starters for when she brought a guy home to make herself look intelligent. While I loved reading about the wonders of the world and beyond, it was just another thing that made me wonder how Cherry and I had ended up staying such close friends over the years.

I knew the answer of course to why we'd become friends... after *They* came to Earth and my parents vanished, I questioned what I had left to fight for after losing everything. The city of New York fell into chaos, everyone stealing and ransacking homes in their panic over the invasion. I found myself trapped in a grocery store one day, while outside, an angry mob of frightened people attacked anyone in their path. They were burning down the stores. And there, in the candy aisle I found Cherry, hiding amid the licorice, crying. I took her hand and together we found a way out through the rear of the store. Guess we'd stuck together ever since out of the pure terror we'd shared. She once told me she'd be my sister and stay by my side always. And I'd been clinging onto that hope ever since, making excuses for all of her shortcomings because I didn't want to be alone. But lately it'd been harder to ignore everything, and I'd found myself questioning her behavior.

Just thinking about those chaotic times sent a chill racing down my spine.

It's the end of the world, everyone had screamed. Panic spread like wildfire across the world, lasting months.

Soon after, the Vepar had broadcasted their rules for our

behavior and how everyone who broke them would be punished. No stealing. No killing. Return to our normal lives or else, they insisted. No one knew what the consequences entailed, but when more and more of us went missing, it didn't take long for people to catch on that those who disappeared never came back. Order returned fast to our lives; order born of fear. And then the other rules came into force about females registering regularly, for us to exercise daily, and so on. No explanations, just orders of what to do next like we were being prepared for something big.

I shook my head at the direction my thoughts had taken and took a step forward in Cherry's apartment through the hazy air. There was a thick cloud of smoke that assaulted my senses and it grew thicker as I moved deeper into the apartment, making me cough. There were people everywhere in her living room dancing and drinking. So many people spilled out onto her balcony, overlooking the city. The dance music thumped so loud that it seemed to pound the inside of my skull.

Cherry was sitting on a guy's lap on the couch in her living room, a contraband cigarette in her hand. I noticed that the man she was rubbing herself all over was not the one she'd said she spent the week with or one that I recognized from the club. It was another man she must have picked up. He was tall and lanky with short hair and was pretty ordinary looking. Very unlike the usual dates she picked - all muscles and gorgeous. I just stared at her for a second not believing that while I was having the worst few weeks of my life, she apparently had been partying it up with a crowd of strangers that I had never seen before.

"Cherry," I finally yelled, straining to be heard over the music and the loudness of the party guests.

She looked up at me after I had called out her name a

few times. It had to be my imagination but when she first looked up at me it almost looked as if she was annoyed to see me. The expression faded so fast that I couldn't be sure what I had just seen.

"Ella," she said, in the fakest voice I had ever heard from her.

"Can I talk to you?" I asked, letting the desperation I was feeling leak into my voice. She stood slowly, whispering something into her guy's ear, a man that upon closer inspection looked extremely greasy and disgusting. I couldn't imagine where she'd picked him up at.

I started walking towards Cherry's bedroom, looking back every few seconds to make sure she was still following me. There were people everywhere and they all seemed to be closely acquainted with my best friend. One guy we passed even managed to stop Cherry and stick his tongue down her throat before she could follow me again.

I gave a little screech when I walked into her bedroom and there was the guy Cherry had picked up at the Vepar club, balls deep in another girl on Cherry's bed of all places. I expected Cherry to look annoyed, but she just laughed when she saw them. "I need you to move the party somewhere else, baby," she cooed at the couple who seemed to be even more enthusiastically going at it with an audience watching them.

Looking up at Cherry, the creep grinned and pulled out of the girl, not having any problem with the fact that he was butt naked in front of Cherry and me. He took the girl's hand and pulled her out of the room, both still naked, shooting a cheeky grin at Cherry as he passed us.

I eyed the bed and shivered in distaste. It was looking less and less likely that I was going to be able to stay here. And since when was Cherry into swinging?

"What do you need me for?" she snapped at me. "I obviously have stuff going on right now," she continued, not sounding shamed at all over the fact that she was having a giant party that she had failed to tell her best friend about. Not that I'd attend such a sleazy affair, but it was the principle of not being invited.

I let that argument drop just as I did about everything else in our friendship that made me upset.

"I need help," I told her.

Cherry's face remained unchanged at my pronouncement, so I continued. "There are three Vepar that have been following me ever since that night at the club. They're literally everywhere, Cherry. I can't get rid of them and I'm scared about what they're going to do to me. Can I stay here for a little while just until I can come up with a plan?" My breath raced as I waited for her to answer.

Cherry burst out laughing, the kind of laughter that would make anyone cry a little at the fact that someone was laughing so hard at them.

"Three Vepar are following you?" she gasped. "Where do you even come up with this stuff?"

Fire climbed over my neck and cheeks. "I'm telling you the truth!" I snapped

"Oh, honey," she said with a disdainful glance. "If you're jealous that I haven't been talking to you this week, this isn't the way to get my attention back with some made up story. I'm allowed to have other friends." Her voice rose in anger, and she gripped her hips.

I looked at her shocked, my mouth hung open. "You can't honestly believe I'd make this up?" I whispered.

With a raised chin, she began to walk away from me. "I have guests to get back to. You know the way out, don't you?"

she asked in a condescending voice as she disappeared from view out the bedroom door.

I sank onto her bed in disbelief before quickly jumping up when I remembered what I'd just witnessed happening on the bed. I slowly made my way back through the party to the front door, taking one last look at my best friend who was now making out with one guy while the one from the club finished his business with his lady friend on the couch next to them - in full view of everyone. Who the hell were these people Cherry was mixing with?

While part of me toyed with the idea of dragging her out here and getting her to open her eyes to what she was doing, I also felt betrayed. An ache curled around my heart, squeezing it tight, reminding me that this wasn't the first time Cherry had let me down.

More than anything though, I felt hopelessness as I stepped out of the building into the night. The rain came pouring down in sheets, drenching me to my bones in seconds and fitting my mood perfectly.

What was I supposed to do next?

I couldn't go home and keep putting up with the Vepar following me. But I also didn't want to sleep on the streets. Looking around, I remembered that there was a small motel a few blocks away that we had stumbled across one night when I was trying to herd a drunk Cherry home. Thinking of the money the Vepar had dumped on the table in the cafe, I decided that wouldn't be a bad option.

A night or two of being alone, hidden, without having to be afraid sounded amazing. Maybe I'd splurge and get myself a big tub of chocolate ice cream and drown myself in it. I hugged my backpack to my chest, trying to keep it as dry as possible, and ran down the sidewalk in the direction of the hotel. The rain fell in chaotic directions, and the violent wind slammed into me making the walk seem ever longer than it really was.

This was turning into quite the night. Not only had my friend turned her back on me, and three Vepar were following me, but now I was stuck in a crazy thunderstorm. I just hoped I wasn't hit by lightning.

The rain fell hard and diagonal as if it meant to wash me away. It pelted into the sidewalk, knocking into buildings, roofs, and cars. Water splashed up to my knees, drenching my sneakers, making each step make a squishy sound. But I kept going past the store fronts and fancy hotels, watching as my surroundings became seedier and seedier. People darted past me, hiding under umbrellas and staring at me with pity, but I kept going, because in that moment, I felt pity for myself too. For my friend letting me down, for the fact that I had to run away at all. I wanted to scream at Cherry, maybe even throttle her. She had been a bitch tonight, and I was right back where I always was...taking care of myself.

After popping into a convenience store to grab a frozen meal and some snacks, I turned right at the next street corner where the storefronts grew sparse and walked towards the neon light of a sign flashing that vacancies were open at the Palace Motel.

This place was anything but regal. A three-story, concrete building was surrounded by a parking area filled with weeds growing out of the cracks in the path. Metal stairs were visible, leading up to the various floors. I somehow doubted the safety inspector had visited this place in years.

A young couple were drunkenly swaying as they ran up the path toward the stairs through the rain. I did the same, targeting the reception door. I burst inside and shut myself in while water dripped down my face and clothes creating a small puddle on the floor beneath me. Even my underwear was soaked.

I turned around to the large reception room. The counter on the right had an older woman picking at her nails, and on the left sat a dusty couch where two men in silky shirts and jeans lounged, legs wide, their eyes all over the newcomer. Me.

Ignoring them, I swung toward the receptionist and made hasty steps toward her.

She glanced up, still cleaning her nails. "How many nights?"

"Umm." I tottered on my feet, unsure how long I planned to stay when I had limited funds and just needed some time to think things through. Check out would be 10am and I wasn't working tomorrow, so I could at least hide here all day. "Two nights please," I finally said.

"$172 for two nights. Towels are in your room." She swiveled on her stool and picked a random key from the wall of hooks behind her before tapping something into the computer on the side.

I dug into my bag, juggling the bag of food, and pulled out two bills. I slid them across the counter holding my breath that she wouldn't ask for a credit card.

The fact that I was paying in cash didn't even faze her. Evidently this was the type of establishment where that was commonplace. She didn't even ask me to show her my license. Once she examined the cash, apparently checking to make sure it wasn't counterfeit, she handed me my change and the key on a ring with a tag for my room number.

"Number 222. Just give the door a jiggle as it gets stuck when it rains. Have a pleasant stay." Her smile was anything but genuine... it belonged on someone bored and exhausted. And who could blame her when this was where she had to spend her time. I could only imagine the type of things she had to deal with here.

"Thanks." I smiled and collected my belongings before turning toward the glass door. Outside, the deluge continued, and I tucked the key and money into my pocket, before reaching for the door. A shadow fell over me from behind.

Thinking I'd forgotten something, I turned, expecting the lady from the counter. Instead it was one of the men from the couch, wearing a purple silky shirt, open half-way to showcase his hairy chest. He smiled with yellowing teeth, even though he looked to be in his late twenties. He really should take better care of himself, but I somehow doubted he'd appreciate me suggesting he brush at least twice a day.

"You got an appointment tonight?" he asked, slouching against the faded wall with his hands in the pockets of his jeans, while he stared at me with a sly grin. His gaze trailed up and down my soaking wet body.

An Appointment? I had no idea what he was talking about.

"I need to get to my room," I said, turning back around as two young girls, maybe eighteen or nineteen, rushed inside with an umbrella they shared. A massive man followed them, clearly some kind of guard for the women.

I stepped back as they splashed water everywhere, including on me.

"Bitches," the guy snapped. "You're getting me fucking wet."

They sneered but never said a word as they rushed over to the other man by the couch, taking a seat on either side of him. They all chatted in whispers, and only then did I realize they most likely were hookers and these guys were pimps.

"So?" The purple shirt guy asked. "You up for a fun night? I'll get you a warm meal." He glanced down at my bag with its microwaveable chicken meal, chips, and tub of ice cream. "And some fresh clothes. We can all do with a fresh start. I'll have your back." He sniffled and rubbed the back of his hand under his nose.

Fresh start. Yes, that was exactly what I needed. I had to stop fooling myself that I'd ever get ahead in my current life, especially with three Vepar on my heels. I knew exactly what I had to do over the next two days. Come up with a plan to leave this city, maybe the state. Relocate to a small town where things were cheaper, where I could keep to myself. Maybe I'd explore getting a job at a school or something better than a cafe. I'd start an online course to get ahead and be able to demand better pay. And a small town would probably have fewer Vepar...or hopefully no Vepar.

I didn't know where a place like that existed, but I had two days to work out a complete rehaul of my life.

"Yo, you're being fucking rude, just ignoring me." His voice climbed, but I didn't have time for him.

"Thanks for your insight," was all I said, gaining myself a confused glare. I ignored his attempt at further conversation, and I darted outside where the ferocious wind and rain once again hammered into me.

Within minutes, I stepped into room 222 and slammed the door shut behind me, quickly locking the two flimsy locks available on it. A new sense of excitement and nerves coaxed my pulse into a race. I was doing this finally... making a change I'd been pondering for months. Sure, I just earned a new job, but what good was that if the Vepar were planning on kidnapping me, or whatever they had planned? I'd start new. I'd done it before, and I could do it again.

I switched on the light to see a small room with a double-sized bed against the one wall, brown patchy carpet, and a round table with chairs at the back. Nearby stood a small counter with a coffee machine, packets of coffee, filters, and several cups. Looking around I found a microwave on the bathroom counter. Perfect.

It was a crappy room, but somehow it didn't feel as terrible as it could. Here I didn't have to look over my shoulder wondering when the Vepar were going to show up next.

I dumped my bag on the table and prepped my frozen meal, starting the coffee maker up too so that I could help myself warm up. I then stripped off my wet clothes and pulled on the folded robe I found in the bathroom.

Yep, tonight was the start of a new beginning. I giddily picked up the ice cream and plastic spoon that I had gotten from the store and ripped off the lid. For once, I was going to try doing things differently, starting with eating dessert first. I dug into the ice cream and pushed aside the worried thoughts that somehow the Vepar would track me down no matter where I went. If I thought like that, I might as well give up right now.

6

$\mathcal{W}$aking up felt like I was treading through a fog, I couldn't quite get to my destination. I shifted in and out of consciousness for what felt like days. Strange voices flitted around me, liquid was slipped down my throat, I could feel someone touching my hair...but still I slept on.

When I finally emerged from my deep sleep, it felt like I'd been sleeping for years. There was sunlight streaming in from a large window to my right that took up almost the whole side of the room...a very unfamiliar room I might add. This wasn't my place or the seedy motel.

Panicking, I tried to rack my brain for where I was. Had I gone out with Cherry and gotten drugged? Sleepwalked? Was I still dreaming? A million different scenarios ran through my head until I fell on one that filled me with the most dread of all.

They'd taken me.

The Vepar.

The strange three men who'd been following me around for weeks.

Sitting up in bed, I was relieved to see that for the moment, I was at least by myself in a giant bedroom easily twice the size of my loft. I sat in the largest bed I'd ever seen, easily able to fit four sleeping adults. Moving my legs, I noted that the silky sheets were also the nicest I'd ever felt as they slid against my skin. Wherever I was, the person who owned this place owned expensive things. And if I was kidnapped, this had to be the strangest prison I'd ever seen.

Looking down at myself, I found myself wearing a flimsy white nightgown. My brain started to short circuit as I realized I wore nothing underneath, meaning that someone had taken off my bra and underwear and had seen everything.

Dread crept over me at the thought of what they'd done to me while I lay unconscious, but as I shuffled out of the bed, I sensed no pain, and especially not the kind I'd expect between my thighs if someone had forced themselves on me. Someone had broken into the motel room, carried me away without anyone noticing, redressed me, then laid me to sleep in a bed that would have belonged in a real palace. Not the run-down motel Palace.

I had to be dreaming.

But if it was the Vepar, and at this point that seemed the most likely scenario, how the hell had they found me at the motel?

Getting out of the bed, I walked on shaky legs to the window to look out and find my location. I gasped at the forest that spread out in front of me for as far as the eye could see. No sign of the skyscrapers that usually graced my eyesight. Wherever I'd been taken, it was a long way from home. My heart beat like it was trying to escape, matching my situation perfectly because I was about to have to try and escape.

A lock clicked behind me, and I backed into the corner, looking around wildly to see if there was anything, I could use to defend myself.

The door cracked open and an older, plump woman opened the door. Her silvery hair fell to her shoulders. "Oh good, you're up," she said cheerfully as if we knew each other. She started bustling around the room, going over to the bed and beginning to straighten the sheets.

Adrenaline flooded my body, and I bolted through the door she'd left open.

I heard her say, "Oh, dear," as I left the room, but no footsteps followed me to signal she was trying to stop me.

A flight of stairs lay a ways down the hallway, and I flew down them not sure what I was going to do if the Vepar were waiting for me down below. I just knew that I couldn't stay still any longer.

I jumped the last few steps, landing on the wooden floorboards with a loud creak. They were cold beneath my feet, icy almost. I glanced around to the open kitchen I'd entered, flooded in bright sunlight that was pouring in from the enormous windows. Everything was sleek lines, white, and very clean. The L-shaped counter was made of white marble, peppered with the latest kitchen gadgets including a mixer, stainless steel coffee machine, juicer, blender, and mini oven. The sweetest aroma of pancakes found me, and my stomach betrayed me, gurgling with hunger as I realized I didn't remember ever getting to my frozen meal last night. I stared at the stack of pancakes on the island counter accompanied by an array of syrups and cream and chopped fruit. I couldn't remember the last time I'd eaten something so decadent. I obviously wasn't going to get to eat it this time either.

Footfalls sounded upstairs, and I spun on the spot, searching for a way out. There on my right, stood a slightly open door with what seemed like sunlight shining out of it. A way out!

Adrenaline coursed through me, and I sprinted forward. When I dragged the door open wider, I ran straight into someone solid as stone. Stumbling backward, I whimpered, staggering over my feet, only to notice someone darting forward from the doorway to capture the mountain of blueberries that had flipped out of the bowl in his hand. Tiny purple balls rained down on me.

I fell on my ass, the tiny fruit tapping the floor around me. I looked up in dismay to see the blond haired Vepar who'd been following me around in the black town car studying me with a raised brow from the doorway.

"Going somewhere?" he asked in an amused tone. He was wearing nothing but a pair of loose pajama bottoms that hung low, showing off that "v" line that every girl seemed to be obsessed with. I hadn't thought that it really existed before now, and I couldn't stop staring. I had to stop.

He glanced down at the blueberry covered floor. "Guess we'll have to have strawberries this morning," he said with a sigh, beginning to walk past me, not bothering to pick up the blueberries or help me off the floor. I stared after him, my mouth hanging open in shock. I stood shakily and turned to bolt again for the door.

"There's nowhere for you to run, my pet," came another voice right as I took my first step. Moving toward the door I was about to run towards was the dark haired Vepar who seemed to be everywhere in my life recently.

"Where am I?" I asked in a trembling voice, suddenly very much aware of how thin my nightgown was. He took a step closer, his gait smooth and predatory. That was a trait of the Vepar that had always scared me, everything about their movements were a little too fluid, a little too perfect...a little too inhuman.

The Vepar studied me, not answering my question. He was dressed in jeans and a tight-fitting black t-shirt that went well with the bad boy image he had going for him. I could see the hint of a tattoo peeking out from the top of his shirt.

"Bring her in here," the other Vepar called from the kitchen. As the black haired Vepar in front of me took another step closer, I panicked, my fight or flight instincts taking full effect. I had already tried the flight, apparently now it was time for the fight. I flew at the Vepar, scratching and clawing all the skin I found, shrieking as I did so like I was possessed.

Suddenly his hand encircled my neck in an iron grip, cutting off my air flow so abruptly that I couldn't breathe. I tried to claw at his hands, but I might as well have been a child swatting at him with how little of a difference it made.

Leaning in close to me, he whispered in my ear, "Are you done yet, pet?"

I was just about to pass out, all the fight drained out of me, when he abruptly let me go. I flopped to the floor, squishing several of the blueberries underneath me as I fell. Footsteps sounded behind me.

"Pick her up and bring her here," the blonde haired Vepar snapped. I felt myself being picked up by the waist and something that almost felt like a caress across my hair calmed me as I walked. Had that been in my imagination?

The black haired Vepar set me down in a chair way more gently than I thought he was capable. Still trying to recover from my momentary strangling session, I stared at my surroundings, keeping the two Vepar who were now both watching me in my sights as I did so.

It was clear I was in some sort of home, and not just a house, the nicest place I'd ever been to. There were at least five doors leading from the kitchen alone now that I looked more closely, making it unlikely that I would have been able to find a way out of this place quickly even if the Vepar hadn't appeared. The mansion looked enormous.

"Hungry?" the blonde asked, setting down a giant stack of pancakes with strawberries on top in front of me. I stared at the food, my stomach growling and making me achingly aware once again that it had not had proper food in a while.

"How long have I been out?" I finally asked as I picked up my fork to take a bite, figuring that I needed to keep up my strength if I was going to get out of here. I also figured that it probably wasn't poisoned since they had gone so far out of their way to kidnap me.

That first bite had me letting out an involuntary groan. It was one of the best things I had ever tasted. Looking up at the two Vepar, I dropped my fork with a clatter. Both of their eyes seemed to be glowing as they looked at me in a way that made it seem like they were more interested in eating me than they were the pancakes. I racked my brain trying to think if I had ever heard rumors that they liked to eat humans. I couldn't think of anything I had heard, but their looks didn't seem normal.

"Make that noise again," said the black haired Vepar, and all of a sudden, I realized what that look was. It was hunger all right...hunger for my body.

I began to eat again, pretending not to notice the way their eyes were still glowing. This time I ate quietly.

Laughing as if I'd made a joke, the blonde turned back to the stove where he was flipping pancakes.

"You cook?" I blurted out as he expertly tossed one in the air, catching it on his spatula smoothly like he was a circus performer.

"We got rid of the help before you woke up," he said dryly, turning to look at me. "I didn't want you scaring them with your antics."

I flushed, cold rage seeping into my veins. "My antics," I said in a low voice. "You mean the fact that I acted like any normal human being would when they were being stalked and then kidnapped by aliens," I snapped.

The black haired Vepar threw back his head and started laughing boisterously. Apparently, I amused them. "The little lamb has some bite after all," he said through his laughter, sounding almost proud of me. Even the blonde was looking at me with a different glint in his eyes. I could tell that it took a lot to faze or impress him, and for some reason that glint gave me a warm feeling inside that I did my best to ignore.

I set my fork down after I realized I'd consumed my entire plate. "What are your names?" I asked, trying to continue the brave front I had briefly put on. "I think it's only fair that I know who's been stalking me for the past few weeks."

"I'm Thane and pretty boy here is named Derrial," the black haired Vepar responded, gesturing to the blonde. It was a relief to have names to attach to their faces. I couldn't keep identifying them by their hair color forever. Though the idea of calling them hottie one, hottie two, and hottie three had crossed my thoughts.

"And the brunette guy who liked to stalk me in the gardens...What's his name?" I asked, knowing he had to be around somewhere. Thane looked like he wanted to laugh but he kept himself in check. "Wonder boy's name is Corran," he said.

"Wonder boy?" I asked.

"He's the lead scientist for the Vepar on Earth," said Derrial. "One of the most brilliant scientists to be born in our society in over a millennium."

I had a million more questions to ask based on his statement alone, but I kept myself in check, trying to focus on the essentials. And it also made sense now why Corran had said that weird stuff about plant species and that Russian village. He'd done his research on Earth and knew a hell of a lot more than I did.

"Why have you been following me?" I asked.

Derrial set the spatula down and leaned back against the counter. "A little bet at first. Who could sleep with the scared, beautiful human first...but after we had all watched you for a while...it just became more. And there's something about you that makes us need to find out why you've got us so curious. So, we knew we had to have you."

I pushed my chair back, standing on legs that were once again trembling, pushing a loose strand of hair behind an ear.

"You started to stalk me as a bet?" I asked in a whisper, my pulse racing and my knees weakening. "I've been terrified. I haven't slept in weeks. I left my whole life behind to try and escape you. What kind of monsters are you?"

"I told you that it changed for us eventually," said Derrial in a nonplussed voice. He began to stalk towards me in a way that left me feeling like prey he was about to catch. At the same time, Thane walked out of the room.

"Stay away from me," I whimpered, backing up until I hit the wall and couldn't go anywhere else. I desperately looked around, praying that someone would appear to help me. But there was no one around. Even the lady upstairs had evidently been sent home.

He didn't stop approaching me until he was pressed up against me. I hated myself when heat spread all over my body from his close proximity.

He was tall, so tall that the top of my head only came to his shoulder despite the fact that I'd never been considered a short girl. And his scent... I swallowed hard, burning up at how sexy he smelled. A combination of muskiness and the crisp freshness of the outdoors. It was a pleasant scent that in a strange way calmed me and slowed my racing heart.

"You're safe with us," he murmured as if struggling to find his words while we were pressed together. I was no fool to know what he struggled with. The bulge in his pants nudged against my lower stomach... He was huge. The corners of his mouth tugged upward, well aware of what I felt.

I wasn't sure if I should be scared or turned on as I pictured him naked and what something that size could possibly do to me in the bedroom. An inferno climbed through me, but I pushed the vision away alarmed at my thinking. It was wrong and distracting when I was here as their prisoner, not their lover.

I didn't move. I didn't dare. For all I knew, they had a basement filled with humans in cages they experimented on. The whole Area 51 and aliens came to mind, especially since, as ironic as it sounded, the reporters had said the first alien vessel to make an appearance on Earth was over Area 51. Funny. At least the UFO believers had gotten something right. What they got wrong was everything else...

Derrial studied me as if he could read my thoughts. What exactly had he meant by being curious about me? I was as plain Jane as they came. I led a boring life, followed the rules, end of story. If they wanted interesting, they should look up Cherry.

"I don't think the word, *safe*, has the same meaning to you as it does me," I responded.

Derrial blinked slowly, and I was caught in the perfection of his blue eyes, his lashes were so long and thick any girl would have been jealous. Up close his pupils were a mosaic of blues, like crystalline waters, and for a few moments I wanted to fall into them.

His fingers were like a vise, pressing into my arms as he held me against him, and he stared down at me so intently.

"You're hurting me. Let me go, Derrial." My jaw clenched.

He hauled me toward the enormous window, and I stumbled alongside him before he spun me to look outside. An ocean of pine trees spread out as far as the eye could see, enormous mountains in the distance like sentinels watching over us. Beautiful, but right now it was terrifying as it meant we were alone out here and nowhere near home.

"See that out there?" he said, pointing to the wood covered landscape. I held my breath, preparing for the worst.

"Yeah."

His grip softened and his palms slid down my arms, feather soft. "For miles there's nothing but wilderness, animals, and danger," he whispered in my ear, his breath warm, melting the ice in my veins.

I struggled to concentrate. It was hard to focus on his words when his fingers were skipping across my stomach. The world seemed to be moving in slow motion as he caressed my skin. I couldn't focus on anything but our connection. His rock-hard chest sat flush against my back, his bulge pushing against me, and his hand inched up my stomach ever so slowly.

I gasped for air. "Danger?"

His fingers trailed under my breasts gently, a wisp's touch away from grazing them, only the light fabric of my nightgown between us. Heat pooled between my thighs, and I grew wetter with the anticipation. My breath hitched; my mind focused only on his closeness. My body betrayed me, begging me to turn around and kiss him, discover what a Vepar tasted like. I should have slammed my heel into his foot, instead I stood there, my body thrumming with my racing pulse, my heart in my throat, waiting for him... What was he waiting for?

"There are rumors," he began, his words still hushed, "of escaped *caiks*. Creatures from our world that are akin to your wolves living in these woods. They're carnivores with a sharp beak and tongue, making them ideal for eating creatures. Vicious things that stowed away on a few ships when we arrived." He paused, seemingly for dramatic affect. "So, my advice to you is to not wander out there alone."

"Are you kidding me?" I twisted my head to face him, and his expression remained stoic. "Why would you let them loose on our planet and not round them up? It's your responsibility to not destroy our ecosystem."

Someone cleared their throat, and I glanced over to find it was the Vepar with brown hair, Corran. Clearly the scientist agreed with me.

Derrial's hands disappeared and he backed away, his earlier warmth replaced by a chill from the loss of his body against mine.

Thane broke into a laugh. When had those two come into the room?

I glanced up at Derrial. "You're joking about the *caiks*, right?"

He shrugged, but the edges of his mouth twitched as if he might break into a smile.

Asshole.

"The house is yours to enjoy. We're heading out for a short while." Without another word, the three of them strolled out of the room, and the sound of a door closing reached me.

"What the hell?" I followed them into a hallway containing a chandelier hanging overhead that dripped in crystals and paintings of forests and open land adorning the walls. I rushed to the grand white door that must be the main entrance to the mansion, but it was locked, and I couldn't find any way to unlock it. I felt around thinking there must be some hidden way to open the door, but after half an hour of searching, I gave up. A sinking sensation washed through me. I may not be in a cage, but this was a prison still the same.

If the Vepar were going to lock me up in their home, then they should expect me to do some snooping, not to mention track down a telephone to call for help. Definitely not Cherry after her crap...maybe my new boss at the cafe might help.

I wished I'd spent more time making more friends, socializing, rather than keeping to myself. But I was a fool for too long and believed Cherry was all the friendship I needed as I struggled with losing my parents. I wished I could rely on her, and I kept telling myself maybe she was going through something, struggling with her own things. Maybe I had been the person in the wrong because I hadn't noticed, and I'd never asked her about it. Regardless, her behavior had been horrible, and she really hurt me when I needed her the most. I wasn't sure I was ready to forgive her...or even if it was possible for me to forgive her at all.

Shaking aside my thoughts about Cherry, I returned back to the current pressing need to escape from here. I grabbed one of the stools at the island counter and carried it over to one of the floor-to-ceiling windows. My heart raced; I knew the Vepar would be pissed if they came home to a broken window. But I wasn't staying here if they were going to be stupid enough to leave me alone. With all my strength, I hurled the stool in my hands into the window.

It smacked against the glass with an explosive thud, then bounced backward with such speed that I had to jump out of the way to avoid getting hit. Fear tightened around my chest. The stool rolled and slid across the kitchen floor until it smacked onto the counter and came to a dead stop.

"Shit!"

The window didn't show a single blemish or crack. I walked closer and ran my hand over its smooth surface. They must have some kind of bullet proof glass. This had to be some kind of compound to keep people locked in the house... or something out? Humans hated the Vepar, so they'd have to think there would be someone who'd attack them.

Regardless, unease sat in my stomach because it seemed getting out of here was an impossibility. Still, I spent the next hour checking all the potential exits of the house that I could find.

Finally giving up, I headed back into the kitchen. I opened the fridge, shivering a bit at the chill. The shelves were filled with fruit and vegetables. I grabbed a banana and a bottle of water, then searched every drawer and cupboard. No knives in sight, and I rolled my eyes. No telephone in sight either. I made my way into a room that came off the kitchen. My stomach knotted with anticipation of finding Vepar secrets. In the room I found a King-sized bed perfectly made with black bedding. I padded over to the wardrobe and pulled it open to discover neatly hung clothes. Tailored pants, suits, shirts...This had to be Derrial's room. The room had that tidy, perfectly organized feel to it, and I got the urge to mess something up just to see if he would notice. I controlled myself.

There were no bedside tables or anything else in this room and of course the windows were unopenable, so I took another bite of my banana and rushed into another room, dropping off the peel onto the kitchen counter as I passed through it. I found an in-house gym, filled with weights, and I quickly moved onto the next room as I had no interest in exercising. Another bedroom, simple again with a large bed, tidy once again. The closet held jeans, tees, shirts and a couple of suits only. I fingered the leather jacket, smiling. Okay, someone had taste. The bedside drawers were empty. What the hell... it was as if these men didn't actually live here. Where were their gadgets or anything about their planet... or anything at all? The next room sat empty, and I found no other doors downstairs or even a basement entrance.

Gulping down several mouthfuls of chilled water, I headed upstairs. The bedroom I woke up in lay ahead, the door open, and bright light poured in through the windows. To my right sat two doors. The first one was a bathroom with the largest tub I'd ever seen, possible for three people to share comfortably. The feet were gold just like the small touches on the sink. Opening the cabinets showed nothing but packaged toothbrushes, toothpaste, shampoo and an array of toiletries, plus towels. Everything was expensive, brands that I had only heard of in celebrity magazines but never imagined being able to use on myself. Nothing that could help me to escape or defend myself in any way, however.

The next door sat locked, and I stiffened, then tried the handle a few more times.

"Maybe this is the secret room of mystery." I placed my ear to the door and swore I heard a soft whirring sound as if someone left a fan running. What was in there? Maybe it was where they kept the chocolate and television. I laughed at how unlikely that was, but wishful thinking on my part. I bet they had a telephone in there.

A quick check in the last room had me gasping. Shelves covered three fourths of the room, filled to the brim with books. It was like something out of Beauty and the Beast complete with a window seat that had a cushion, inviting me to sit there and soak in the sun while reading. In the middle sat a round table and three chairs, and I pictured the three Vepar sitting here, discussing new things they found in these books. I hurried inside, forgetting everything else, and ran my hands over the spines of the books, on various topics from governments, inventions, space exploration, and even one on the best slow cooked meals. Interesting. I assumed that belonged to the lady I'd seen earlier making my bed.

Back in the bedroom, I found a pile of clean clothes waiting for me in the closet. Jeans and a frilly blue buttoned-up shirt, which was strange, but they looked about my size. A silky pair of underwear fell out from the shirt and I picked it up, noting how tiny the thong was, and heat crawled up my cheeks, thinking of the men picking this out for me. Had they been planning to bring me here all along, so they bought me clothes? Or was this from another girl who they'd kept a prisoner and she just happened to be my size? If that was the case, what happened to the women once they fell out of favor with these Vepar?

I collected my clothes and marched into the bathroom, needing a shower and non-transparent clothes for when the Vepar returned. One way or another I was going to find out exactly what they wanted from me. And I wasn't taking no for an answer.

7

I stared outside through the window of the library room, at the shadows spreading over the forest as the sun started to descend behind the mountains. Had Derrial been kidding about the alien wolf animals on loose in these woods? I didn't know them well enough to understand when they were joking. But either way, the moment I got a chance to escape, I'd run out of here, ferocious alien animals or not. A little voice in my head reminded me of how easily they'd found me at the motel, but I shook the thought away. I wasn't going to give up now or ever.

My stomach growled, and I made my way downstairs, tying up my long hair into a ponytail, thinking that on the bright side, I didn't need to visit the gym today. I wasn't quite sure what day it was, but I knew that I had work coming up. I thought again how not showing up made my heart ache since everyone there had been so kind to me. I hoped they wouldn't hate me for not being there.

I sighed as I dragged myself down the stairs, remembering Thane's words about me having to give my notice to my job soon. I clenched my hands. Ever since they'd entered our world, they pushed and pushed to control every aspect of our lives but kidnapping me and taking me to their remote home was a whole different level of control. Or was this the beginning of what their kind intended to do to all humans?

I opened the fridge and stared at the food, not in the mood for more fruit and veggies. I opened the freezer and was happy to find several containers of what looked like premade meals, one of them ending up being lasagna. Perfect. I threw it into the microwave and waited. The lights in the kitchen automatically switched on, and I squared my shoulders, listening closely, expecting the Vepar to return. The house remained quiet. I decided the lights must be automated based on the time of the day, so I swung back around to the microwave which had just beeped, signaling my dinner was ready. The aroma had my stomach growling. A little part of me wondered if Derrial had made the food.

By the time I devoured the entire container of food, I reclined back in my seat and sighed. Maybe I had it all wrong and the Vepar intended to kill me with boredom. No television or music, and my bag wasn't anywhere in the bedroom upstairs. Did that mean they left it back in the motel, along with my house keys and cell phone? I hoped not.

An hour later, the front door unlocked, and voices reached me. I climbed to my feet and moved to stand with my back to the floor to ceiling window, waiting, my stomach twisting with the unexpected.

Thane strode into the kitchen first, his piercing blue eyes finding me in an instant. He smiled. "Missed us, pet?"

I didn't respond, but watched as he sauntered closer, followed by Derrial and Corran who both surprised me by offering me warm smiles. They seemed to behave as if this were normal behavior to have a prisoner in their home.

"Where's my handbag?" I blurted out.

"In a safe place," Corran answered, running a hand through his deep brown hair. It brought attention to his strong facial features and the thought crossed my mind how easily he could grace the cover of any magazine and have women all over the world fawn over him. Crazy how I hadn't thought he was as attractive as the others when I first saw him.

I shook my head in disgust at myself. I shouldn't have had to keep reminding myself that these men weren't human, that they might be wearing a disguise. Despite knowing that, I couldn't stop from staring at them in awe, noticing the small things like how Corran had a dimple in his chin when he smiled, how his breathing picked up when he looked at me.

"When do I get to go home?" I glanced from one man to the next, but none of them said a word. They all just stared at me without expression, giving nothing away.

"That's not how this works," Derrial finally broke the silence. "First, you need to understand you are now ours, that you'll never be free." He glanced outside the window, and I followed his line of sight to the gray storm clouds rolling overhead. Something ominous was coming in... I was beginning to believe my grandma more and more about her superstitions on storms.

I gripped my hips as Thane and Corran headed into the kitchen. One began making coffee, the other pawed at something in the fridge. What exactly did Vepar eat anyway? Humans?

"Fine then," I said. "I'm yours. Now, can I go home?"

Derrial burst into a laughter so powerful and loud, it

could have been the thunder booming overhead. I guessed he was mocking me with his chortle once again.

Just sharing the room with these three had me burning up with rage, and I wanted to throw a chair at them. "Why the hell can't you just speak straight and tell me what's going on? Keeping me here is called kidnapping and it's illegal on Earth."

"We have always told you the truth, but you choose not to listen," Corran said, just as he had back in the botanical gardens with his stupid riddles.

I huffed and clenched my teeth, then stormed across the kitchen, my footfalls punching the wooden floorboards. How could I be near these three a second longer when all I wanted was to attack them? I glanced around, needing alone time. I opted for the small library as that place had a similar calming effect on me as the Botanical Gardens. Right now, I needed a bucketload of tranquility to extinguish the inferno in my veins.

I paced back and forth in front of the window, unable to appreciate the gorgeous view outside, unsure if I wanted to cry or scream. What in the world did the Vepar mean by 'understand I was theirs'? Like in a cult? Or was it as simple as starting to show them I accepted their kind in my life, smiled more often, complimented them on their looks and their ideas for the world... I sighed at myself. Clearly, not their looks, but other things. Though I wasn't a fool to believe when they said *ours* it meant simply having them as my friends. I somehow suspected this was far deeper, something to do with the way they lived on their home planet, wherever that was considering they hadn't told anyone, and it was evidently much farther than where humans had been able to travel.

The floorboard creaked behind me, and I spun around

to find Derrial walking through the doorway, closing the distance between us in a few steps. Determination seared his features, his golden hair perfectly framing his face, all tanned skin and high cheekbones.

My heart catapulted to my throat, but I stood there, lifting my chin in defiance even if I trembled all over. I refused to show him any fear.

He was on me in seconds, his body pressed against mine, staring down at me, and his hands clasped my arms hard. I backed away, but he followed until my back hit the wall.

"Let me go," I pleaded, my voice cracking.

He paused for a moment, studying me, and a blaze burned behind his blue eyes. But with the bulge nestled against my stomach, I understood exactly his intention. He held me as he'd done downstairs, except now something else crossed his face as if he barely contained himself from attacking me, and that terrified me.

Was that what they meant by being theirs... offering myself to them without hesitation? With our bodies glued together, and the sheer size and strength of him, I stood no chance to push him away. He'd leave when he wanted to, when he was ready.

"Back on our planet," he began, "when we select a female, it's for life."

I swallowed hard, processing his words. They chose me to be theirs for life? Fuck! So many questions circled my mind, but none of those fell from my lips. "Why me?"

He gripped my chin and lifted my head higher to face him. "You remind me of me, desperate for freedom, never giving up the fight, even when you know there's no way out."

"Then please," I begged, ignoring my curiosity about what freedom he needed. "If you understand, release me."

He was shaking his head before I finished the words, his grip easing from my chin, his hand falling to my shoulder. His fingers grazed the tender spot on my neck. "You're not listening again. There's nowhere to escape. You're safer with us." His voice rose, yet he lowered his touch to my collarbone.

I hiccupped a breath. "Yes, there is." Despite my words, desire swept through me as it had downstairs, twisting my thoughts into knots.

"I can smell your arousal."

Heat crawled up my cheeks, and I shoved my hands into his solid chest, but he wouldn't budge.

His body pushed closer, arms locked around me, his chest rising and falling quickly. The expression over his face was of pure ecstasy and urgency, and when he lowered his mouth to my neck, licking me, my sex clenched. It shouldn't have, but something about him set me on fire.

The pressure built within me, and I loathed that I enjoyed the way his mouth tenderly kissed my skin, how the warmth of his quickened breath covered me in goosebumps. Sweeping up and over my chin, he reached my lips, pressing himself against me. He kissed me softly at first as if testing my response, but something about having such a powerful man needing me undid me.

His hands dropped to my hips and he pulled my lower lip into his mouth, sucking on it, tasting me. I squeezed my thighs together, falling beneath his attention, drowning in desire. I shouldn't want him, I shouldn't be inching my hands up his hard chest, looping them behind his neck, or lifting myself on tippy toes. But I did all that. I was losing myself to a Vepar.

As if my behavior gave him the approval he seeked, he

kissed me faster, taking my tongue into his mouth, a moan brushing over my throat in response.

I kissed him back, desperate to unleash the building pressure strangling me. He reached up and his fingers snagged into my ponytail before pulling out the elastic. My hair fell around me in waves.

He gripped the back of my thigh and placed it around his hip, nudging himself between my legs, taking me, dominating me while we both remained fully clothed.

Was this how we were meant to be? I parted my lips for him, and when he tapped my other leg to wrap it around him too, I held onto his thick arms while he pinned me between himself and the wall. I hated myself for the way I was embracing him between my thighs. His heavy muscles shifted beneath my palms, and I stroked them, but it wasn't enough when I desired skin to skin, to slide over his naked body.

I moaned with desperation, begging for more. All rational thinking disintegrated when he grabbed my ass, rubbing himself against my sex. I pulsed down there in response. He ground faster, his kisses relentless, and sweat collected across my lower back.

Moisture pooled between my legs, breathing came with difficulty, and my nipples ached painfully against my shirt. I'd never had a man dominate me this way.

He grabbed a handful of my hair and yanked my head back as his teeth nicked the flesh of my lip. A coppery taste flooded my mouth, and I winced.

Derrial licked and sucked my wound ferociously as if tasting my blood drove him wild.

He arched my neck back and found my throat, his teeth raking over my flesh, sinking them into my shoulder but not breaking the skin.

I gasped, the pain sharp, but not excruciating. If anything, it flooded me with an excitement, and I moaned for more. I hadn't been with many men, so I didn't have the chance to explore what I enjoyed sexually, but apparently dominant men turned me on.

Pain and desire blended into an emotion I didn't understand, but I wanted more.

I chewed on my cut lip, tasted the metallic blood as it bubbled, but Derrial returned and captured my mouth. A wave of heat engulfed me, shaking me at the core.

"You want this, you live for this," he whispered. "That's why you're ours."

His words sent a deep shock through my soul.

"Derrial," I breathed. I shouldn't have allowed this, should have fought to take back control, should have hurt him.

But I didn't want to, and I groaned again as he continued to rub against my heat. I was dripping wet and squirming beneath him.

His body curled over mine as he ground so hard he left a wake of vibrations over my sex. One minute I brushed the edge, and then I fell in, all my weight wrapped in his arms. I climaxed, convulsing, and my screams muffled against his mouth.

He grunted too, then finally stopped with an unsteady exhale.

Coming up for air, I gasped, not able to find any words for what had just happened. The silence between us grew unsettled after the noise of our moment, but reality slowly slipped through my mind. What had I just done? A tight knot formed in my stomach, making me feel like I was going to throw up.

I wriggled out of his hold, lowering my legs, and he

released me. My knees were jelly beneath me like I walked on a ship deck in a roiling sea, and I had to let the wall hold me up until I found my strength.

Unable to look at the Vepar, I sidestepped past him, wanting to run, to escape, to never see him again as I burned up with embarrassment at how easily I gave myself to him...how my body responded to his. I'd had a freaking orgasm with both of us still dressed.

My body still trembling, I ran toward the parted door from him in shame. And this time, no one came after me.

"Go to your room, little one. Go and tell yourself that I somehow made you like that, that you wouldn't have cum like a bitch in heat if I hadn't forced you," he called after me in a cold, condescending voice.

His words only heightened the shame coursing through my body, and I fled out of the room as fast as I could, not stopping until I got to the room that I had woken up in. I slammed the door behind me, wishing again for some kind of lock on the doorknob.

I backed up until my knees hit the bed behind me, my eyes locked onto the door as I breathlessly waited to see if anyone came after me. Glancing over at my reflection in the window, I stared incredulously at the blood smeared across my chin and neck. Fuck, he'd been tasting my blood... was that what Vepar did? Drink blood?

After five minutes of no one following me, I finally leaned back on the bed, and I cried.

What was wrong with me that I'd let him do that to me? And I actually enjoyed it? What kind of sick person actually delighted in having an alien species that had taken her parents turn her on?

I cried into my pillow for hours, vaguely aware that the fabric beneath my face was a million times softer than the one I slept on in my loft. I cried until I fell asleep. Visions of monsters eating my parents plagued my dreams, and I watched in horror.

When I woke next, night cloaked the room and soft rain pattered against my window. With no clocks in my room and my phone taken from me, I had no way of knowing what time it was. I wasn't going to go downstairs and ask either. I'd rather sit in here forever than face any of the Vepar again.

I felt hopeless as I laid there. This was my life. I had been captured by the same creatures that took my parents, and soon I would disappear just like them. They would either kill me or worse, I would become some sort of human sex slave until I grew too old for them to want me anymore.

Tears threatened again, but I held them in. I would just lay here until they came for me. I wouldn't make it easy on them. They would have to force me to cooperate.

I found myself wishing that they would just kill me.

$\mathcal{I}$t was two days before they came for me. The door crashed open, startling me out of the hazy dreamland I had been in and out of for hours. I felt weak. It had been too long since I'd eaten or drank anything, and I wasn't surprised that the first thing Derrial did was force water down my throat.

"You need to do it slowly," came a voice that I recognized as Corran's.

"She hasn't had anything for too long," snapped Derrial, cursing as he continued to force me to drink water. Two days. I had no idea it had been that long. No wonder I felt so weak.

"Humans shouldn't go without water this long," chided Corran. "Were you trying to kill her?" he asked.

Derrial cursed again. "Would you fucking shut up and get an IV or something," he snapped. "We've all been distracted with pressing shit."

Corran's footsteps sounded as he hurried out of the room. Derrial continued to have me sip water, a look that almost seemed concerned in his too blue to be human eyes.

My stomach rolled, the water too much for my empty stomach. I began to heave, and he hurriedly turned me over on my side as I threw up the water he had just given me.

Corran appeared at that moment holding an IV kit. "Do you know how to do this?" he asked Derrial.

"Get Thane," Derrial snapped, making Corran give him a curious look before he jogged out of the room.

I threw up some more water, soaking the beautiful bed. Derrial softly stroked my hair, pulling it back from my face. "I'm so sorry, beautiful," he whispered, so softly that I could have imagined it.

Thane appeared in the room in what seemed like only a second later. "Is she okay?" he asked in a worried voice.

"I need you to give her this IV," Derrial said in a terse voice that left no room for arguments.

I felt Thane fiddling with my arm, and then a quick prick of pain. "It's in there."

There was silence for a few minutes, then I jumped when there was a crash of glass against the wall.

"She's not to be left alone," cursed Derrial. He then stormed out of the room. I could hear the sound of other pieces of glass breaking somewhere else in the house.

"Stupid, stupid girl," sighed Thane, taking a seat next to me on the bed and absentmindedly stroking my arm. He looked down at me with a pained expression. "Are we really that awful that you would rather give up on life than be with us?"

In all honesty, I didn't know the answer to that because I'd felt so many emotions these past couple of days, I was struggling to wrangle and understand them. How I so easily fell under Darrial's spell, how much I still craved him. I was their prisoner. None of that made sense.

When I didn't answer, he pulled out what looked like a

more high-tech version of the iPhone and started to fiddle with it. I already felt more energized from the IV, yet I struggled to sit up.

"Stay there until the IV is done," Thane barked. "You look like you've somehow managed to lose ten pounds in just the few days you've been up here."

Before I could respond, Corran appeared. He hovered by the door as if he wasn't sure what to do with himself. I watched him for a moment before he seemed to come to a decision. He walked over to the bed and took out a small silver device out of his pocket. When he started to move it slowly along my body, I began to struggle to get away, not sure what alien technology he'd use on me.

"Please, no." I found my voice.

"Calm down," said Thane, putting a little pressure on my arm to still me. "It's just a device that makes sure all of your insides are operating normally."

"You should probably run it over her head too to make sure she doesn't have brain damage," he mused to Corran.

I made a sound of displeasure, and Thane grinned at me.

Corran stepped back after he had run the device all over my body. "She appears to be fine besides being starved and still dehydrated. I'll go get her food," he said, practically fleeing the room as if he couldn't stand to be in my presence for any longer. For some absurd reason, my feelings were a bit hurt at his reaction.

Thane must have seen something on my face. "Don't mind Corran," he said in what I considered a soft voice for him. "He's not that great with your kind, or our kind to think of it. He's more of an observe kind of person. It's actually been shocking at how interested he's seemed in you."

For one stupid moment my mind wandered down the

path of how far Corran's preference for watching went. I quickly shut down that thought when Darrial entered the room carrying the tray of food that I was certain Corran had gone downstairs to get.

Derrial sat on the bed next to me, the mattress dipping under me, and held out what looked like a grilled cheese sandwich. With the energy that the IV gave me, the full brunt of my hunger struck, and I grabbed the grilled cheese out of his hand, practically stuffing it into my mouth.

"Hey...slow down." Derrial dragged the tray out of my reach since I was already reaching for the other half of the sandwich. "You're going to get sick if you eat too fast."

I nodded, forcing myself to slow down. To my disappointment, Derrial set the tray down where I still couldn't reach it and turned to face me. I was suddenly very aware of just how close in proximity Derrial and Thane sat next to me. I'd never had one guy in my bed let alone two aliens. I was reminded as I watched Derrial's eyes glow just who these two were. They may be sweetly taking care of me at the moment, but I couldn't forget that in this situation they were the predators...and I remained the prey.

"We need to come to an understanding." The glow in Derrial's eyes faded as he spoke, seeming to tame whatever inside of him was causing such a reaction. "We're not going to harm you, but you're not going anywhere either. We've been around for too long not to know that there is something about you that's special. And nothing is going to change until we figure out what that is."

I studied him for a moment while he waited for me to answer. I believed him when he said that they weren't going to harm me. I believed him that they believed that. But what they didn't understand was that by taking away everything familiar in my life and forcing me to bend to their will...they were harming me.

"So, what's next?" I finally asked, watching as something that almost looked like relief flashed across his features, softening them.

"Next, you're going to get better," Darrial said, getting up off the bed and handing me the other half of my sandwich. "We're going to the World Summit, and you'll need to be your best as my date."

With that pronouncement he left the room, leaving Thane shaking with laughter next to me.

What the hell was so funny?

THREE DAYS LATER, Corran pronounced me fully recovered and ready to go. Over those last few days there had been an unspoken truce between the four of us. No talking about the Vepar, or my kidnapping. Nothing about why humans went missing apparently either. And no orgasms... Instead we stuck to safe topics like my favorite foods. I found out Derrial loved to cook human food and after he heard that my favorite dishes were Thai, he cooked up a storm and made the most delicious Pad Thai I'd ever tasted in my entire life. We all ate dinner together that night, and I caught their stolen glances my way like they wanted to each steal me away and carry me alone to a room, so they had me all for themselves. The air grew heavy with their need, but I said nothing and enjoyed my food, admiring their self-control. Maybe it was mean of me, but after they turned my life upside down, I bathed in a bit of payback, anyway I could get it.

The whole set up seemed almost normal...Almost...if

having dinner with three of the most gorgeous men in the world constituted as normal.

I stood in front of my walk-in closet, looking through the clothes that continued to appear in there. I wasn't sure how the men were getting access to outfits in the middle of nowhere and how they fitted me perfectly, but at least it had confirmed I wasn't being given clothes from another kidnapped victim since the tags were on every item. Brands that I hadn't imagined I would ever see in real life, let alone get to wear.

Considering I'd been housebound since arriving here I wasn't sure when to wear the ten pairs of Christian Louboutins that were now sitting in my closet. Maybe this trip? Part of me wished I had my phone for the simple reason that I wanted to send a photo of them to Cherry. And that thought made me wonder where she was at. Had she even tried to contact me, and if she had, was she worried at all? What about my new boss? He would have considered me unreliable now and I'm sure my job was long gone. I couldn't go back to working for Greg since I had simply messaged him I was quitting and never showed up again. And I hadn't paid my landlord in weeks, so I'm sure he had started the eviction process for my loft and had probably sold all my belongings. My stomach sunk at the thought, not for my few belongings I had, but for the photos that I had left of my parents that were still at my loft.

Not that I'd accepted my fate here... far from it. But since the Vepar were playing nice, I'd use the opportunity to uncover their real intentions and figure out how to leave in a smarter way.

A knock sounded on my door. After the guys had continued to appear unannounced, I had put my foot down that they had to knock before entering. I was surprised when they actually listened.

"Come in," I called out. It was Derrial, looking so good that it should be a crime in his perfectly fitted grey suit with a black button up and black tie underneath it. His blonde hair had been brushed off his face, falling behind his ears, and I could sit there and stare at him for hours.

"Do you need help packing?" he asked, eyeing the floor with no sign of my bag. I blushed at the thought of this Vepar helping me pack my underwear.

"Maybe just tell me what kind of clothes I'll need, and I can pick them out?" I responded.

"No offense. But I think it's best I select your outfits." He smirked. "In the weeks that we watched you, I don't think I saw you in anything that didn't look like a paper sack. I can tell when a woman is trying to hide herself from the world."

I opened my mouth to object, to say something about my lack of funds, but he was already in my closet tossing things behind him so that they landed on the bed. My eyes widened at the skirt suits and fancy cocktail dresses he picked out.

"What kind of conference did you say this was?" I asked, absentmindedly smoothing out a black, silky dress that I knew was more expensive than six months of the rent for my loft.

"The World Summit," he answered casually, apparently unaware of what effect such an announcement would have on me. When I had heard about the event on the news, I had always imagined the most powerful men in the world sitting around a table in their tailored suits, talking about things I didn't understand. I sighed a heavy exhale at the thought of actually attending the World Summit. Someone like me didn't belong at such a place.

"I can't go with you to that," I squeaked, balling up the aforementioned dress in my hands in distress.

I knew the World Summit was an annual conference held every year in which the leaders of the Vepar and the leaders of various countries in the world met to go over policy and changes that the Vepar wished to implement. Only the most powerful of the Vepar went, making me wonder why Derrial was going to attend. Why would a Vepar powerful enough to represent them at the World Summit have kidnapped a lowly human girl?

When he turned around, holding a glittering gold gown, I took a step back. "What's wrong?" He grinned at me, strolling closer.

"Who exactly are you?" I asked, eyeing him through skeptical lenses. Despite playing happy roommates for the past few days, they hardly revealed anything about themselves, why they were on Earth, why they really took me... nothing to give me some background.

"I guess you'll find out soon." He tossed another blue dress with a flowing skirt onto the bed. "You should have enough clothes right there for the week. Be ready in an hour," he ordered, marching out of the room and closing the door behind him.

I sank to my bed unsteadily. A few days ago, I'd been waiting tables at a small cafe, just trying to make ends meet. Now I was apparently going to wear $20,000 dresses and hobnob with world leaders.

What was happening?

hadn't left the mansion in days, so I was unaware what else surrounded the place aside from what I spotted from the windows down on the grounds. As Derrial led me outside, carrying both of our bags, I spied a giant pool that looked like it could be a miniature water park, and beyond that, what looked like a helicopter pad. Both the pool and the helicopter pad were located behind the building with no view from the windows.

The sound of blades chopping in the wind confirmed that indeed, the Vepar had a freaking helicopter pad complete with helicopter on their property. The chopper landed, and a flurry of winds collided into us, tugging at my hair and clothes. Derrial put his hand on my lower back to guide me forward, sparks erupting down my spine at his touch, responding to his closeness. For days, I'd hated myself for giving in to him so easily, but in truth I was starting to realize that maybe there was more happening between us than me being weak in his presence.

I glanced backwards, expecting Thane and Corran to be somewhere nearby watching us leave, but there was no sign of them. For some reason, I felt disappointed that they hadn't offered me a farewell, but I immediately cursed at myself, wondering if I was beginning to develop Stockholm Syndrome or something.

We climbed into the helicopter and buckled up in our seats. There were two attractive, mountain man staffed with guns, wearing all black, sitting on one side of the helicopter. Great...more Vepar. I glanced over at Derrial, offering him my confused look. Once we placed our ear protectors on, which were complete with microphones and listening devices, Derrial explained that it was customary for all of the leaders to bring armed guards even though it would be suicide to try to hurt any of the Vepar attending.

I stared outside as the country flew underneath, trying to work out where exactly the mansion was located. Derrial's arm was on my thigh and he squeezed my hand to look at him, and he shook his head as if reading my thoughts. I swallowed hard and looked over at the two guards who were studying me. What would they do if I ripped my hand free from Derrial? Probably nothing as I suspected Derrial wouldn't accept it well.

So, I sat there, obediently, still unsure why he insisted on taking me on this trip. An hour into the trip and my ass numb from the vibrating seat, my stomach lurched as we started our descent. I gripped my seat, and Derrial took my hand, holding me.

It wasn't everyday a girl got to travel in a helicopter. Once we landed, jostling us about, the door slid open and the whirring sound of the blades overhead grew deafening. Wind whistled inside, ripping at my ponytail with its invisible hand. The guard stepped out first, followed by Derrial, who turned around and extended his hand to me.

Leaning over, I accepted his help, and once I reached the

doorway, he grabbed my waist and helped me down. We hunched low from the spinning blades, Derrial took my hand, and we rushed across the tarmac, buffeted against the gust of air across our backs.

Finally, we slowed down, and I looked at the small building ahead of us, along with noting that this wasn't a major airport, but a private location surrounded by a chained fence. The guards carried our bags and flanked our sides, and up ahead waited a black limousine with two more muscled men in black. One of them had the back-seat door opened for us, everything creating a million more questions about who exactly Derrial was. It was obvious that I had misjudged just who these Vepar were. Again, I wondered what they were doing with me?

Once we were inside the car that smelled strongly of vanilla, a glass of champagne was pushed into my hand and we were off. Across from us sat two of the guards, both of them staring outside at the freeway we'd entered, while Derrial swirled the ice in his whiskey around in his glass.

"Is this normal travel for you?" I asked and took a sip of my bubbly, which was slightly sweet and tickled my nose.

I'd once tasted this stuff, but clearly it wasn't the good stuff, because this drink was incredible. I downed it in two gulps, and Derrial collected my glass before tucking it into a compartment in the door.

"I prefer to travel lighter," he replied, and shifted in his seat, obviously uncomfortable. In a strange way, it made me feel better to know it wasn't just me feeling like a fish out of water. Was this how he felt all the time on Earth? Knowing everyone around him hated his kind?

"You don't like this?" He glanced over at me; his eyebrow cocked as if disappointed.

I shrugged. "Hard to compare when I don't even have a

car." The laugh that followed my statement felt forced, and part of that was because being so close to Derrial still left me confused. My emotions were a jumbled mess around him. I couldn't stop thinking of how easily he brought me to climax, how damn much I loved it, and even how I'd experienced a dream with him taking me again and again. I was being a fool.

He was a Vepar. Dangerous. Secretive. Not to mention my freaking kidnapper.

I had to get my head screwed on right and remember what was going on.

I was the victim who would pretend to be content with the current situation while waiting for an opportunity to escape. Sure, I hadn't worked out the finer details of how I'd avoid them once I did run away, but that was my goal now-- uncover their weakness, what made them tick, and how to vanish from their lives for good. Until then, I'd bide my time and make them trust me.

"You okay?" he asked, staring at me, trying to read my thoughts, but I smiled widely.

"All good." And I turned toward the window and stared out into the world as we passed it by. A world that seemed so far away from me and out of my grasp that I felt like the alien. I hoped that when I did escape, I would be able to find a place again.

A SOFT VOICE sang in my ear. "Wake up, kitten. We're here."

My eyes fluttered open, still in the back seat of the limousine. Sitting up and looking around I saw that we were parked in the front of some kind of building. I rubbed my eyes as someone opened the door and I climbed out onto the sidewalk, Derrial on my heels. A soft breeze swished past, bringing with it a cocktail of smells from the garlic aroma of pizza to the subtle scent of aftershave coming from the concierge standing near me.

"This way ma'am."

I didn't move though because I was captivated, lost in the grandeur of the hotel towering in front of us. Glass doors stood ahead of us with a young man welcoming us with a bow. He opened the door, while two other men in penguin suits rushed to collect our bags from the trunk.

Derrial placed his hand on my lower back, urging me to move, and I let him guide me through the doors into a circular hotel lobby. Visiting hotels wasn't something I did regularly or ever. Reception sat in front of a set of gorgeous steps that curled up around the wall to the next floor. My boots tapped the shiny floor, and I spun on the spot, taking in the glorious surroundings, the loft ceilings, the guests in their expensive clothes, the way everyone whispered when they talked. I'd never even set foot in such a place, let alone even fathomed staying in one.

Derrial was talking to a man in a tailored black suit and moments later he strolled over to me, smiling. "Ready, kitten?" He handed me his hand to take, so I did, and we made our way to the elevator, the guards following us every step of the way.

By the time we reached the top floor, butterflies somersaulted in my stomach. I shouldn't have been excited, but I was so giddy I could scream.

"Is this the penthouse?" I might have squeaked a bit.

Derrial tapped his card to the door lock and opened it for me, staring at me with the widest grin.

I rushed past him and into a room three times the size of my entire apartment. More rooms stretched out in every direction. Sunlight flooded the penthouse through the enormous windows, reminding me of the kind on store-fronts, so high I felt as if I floated on air.

A bird flew past the window almost as a reminder that we were almost in the clouds. Expensive looking beige couches adorned one end of the room, near the biggest television I'd seen. Bowls of fruit and chocolate, along with more champagne filled the tables. I wasn't sure where to look first, but I ran to the window, pressed up against the glass and looked down. The city lay so far away as if it were another world, the people looked like ants on the sidewalks below.

"We need to get ready quickly," Derrial said.

I turned to him, noting how he studied me with a grin despite his words. "You'll have time to admire the room later."

"Can't I stay here while you go to the Summit?" I'd watch television and eat everything in sight.

He shook his head. "Get dressed in the skirt and jacket suit you packed and bring the black cocktail dress and heels with you. We leave in ten. And if anyone asks, you're my assistant." Without another word, he marched into one of the other rooms, so well versed in the penthouse's layout that it was obvious he'd been here before.

I nodded, even though only the guards watched me, and headed into the hallway where I found my bag sitting on a queen poster bed. If I needed to play the part of assistant or girlfriend for a few days while living here, well, I'd have to find a way to get through it. Either way I couldn't wipe the smile from my face that I was in a freaking penthouse.

Today would be a day of sitting back and looking pretty, playing eye candy on the Vepar's arm, which I could do if it proved to him I was happy to be theirs. A few days could be enough to get him to let his guard down and give me a chance to escape.

Hours later, and the day dragged. Holding back my yawns grew harder and harder. Here I assumed I'd sit in on the World Summit and learn who exactly Derrial was and what the Vepar were doing on Earth, but instead, Derrial hardly had said a word. He sat in a room amid a large circular table, joined by heads from around the world, listening to their concerns and how they intended to work with the Vepar. I almost choked on laughter as each of them tried to appease Derrial. I sat behind him in a wooden chair that numbed my entire body, attempting to play the role of an assistant by sitting there doing nothing.

Being disappointed was an understatement. Why did he want me to attend the Summit anyway?

Once the event ended, I was on my feet, ready for the cocktail party, but that was an even bigger let down. I spent the night with guards surrounding me, and I ate every hors d'oeuvres that was brought my way as I watched Derrial talk to everyone in the hall decorated with overelaborate vases of flower bouquets. Inconsequential polite conversation, wine, and a light orchestra filled the room. This wasn't what I would call a party.

I stepped toward Derrial but a guard grabbed my arm and shook his head when I turned to face him. Right. My place was to sit. Or stand quietly by myself. To be invisible.

Derrial glanced my way and smiled, raising his glass to me. I raised my brow.

On the inside I was ready to scream. Especially since the black stilettos I wore pinched my toes.

After the party, Derrial led me out to the street, what felt like a thousand eyes watching us as we walked out of the ballroom where the cocktail party was being held. We got to the curb as our driver pulled up in the black town car we were using for the week. Derrial opened the door for me but didn't follow me in.

"You're not coming?" I asked, looking up at him and feeling strangely lonely at the thought.

"I have another meeting to attend. I thought you would want the break," he answered, taking a step back from the car and beginning to close the door. He stopped for a second and leaned back in, an irrational part of me thought he might kiss me goodbye.

"Don't bother trying to get away," he said. "Our driver is highly trained and will be walking you back to our rooms and there will be guards stationed outside." With that ugly pronouncement he closed the door, not bothering to look back as he strode away in that smooth, predatory way of his.

As we drove away, I thought for a second of at least trying to get away, but I was so tired after the day of meetings that I immediately abandoned the idea. Especially when it meant dealing with the muscle heads guarding me. Once we arrived at the hotel, where I was indeed marched up to my room by the driver whose name I found out was Dan, I found myself on the news channels watching their interpretation of the Summit proceedings. There was a lot that I had apparently missed. One thing was for sure, all eyes were on Derrial. His face flashed across the screen repeatedly and I wondered how I had stuck my head in the sand so much these past years to not realize he was someone big for the Vepar. I fell asleep watching the news, barely realizing when a strong pair of arms that I vaguely recognized as belonging to Derrial, picked me up and took me to bed.

~

I WOKE to someone nuzzling my hair. I sat up in bed with a start, looking around frantically for who had been touching me. Looking behind me, I saw Derrial lounging near me in nothing but a pair of tight fitting briefs that left little to the imagination. He had a sleepy look on his face that still somehow managed to make him insanely gorgeous.

"Did you sleep in here last night?" I asked, quickly taking a peek at my body to be sure I remained dressed.

"Do you really care if I did?" he asked, an insolent grin on his face. For a brief moment I allowed myself to remember that minute before I had fully woken up, what it had felt like to be enveloped in his arms. And then I quickly pushed the thought away.

"I didn't give you permission to do that," I snapped, getting out of bed. His grin only grew wider.

"I'm pretty sure we've established I never ask for permission," he replied, also getting out of bed. I averted my eyes from all of his perfect golden skin and rushed out of the room. "Be ready in twenty minutes," he called after me. "I have an important meeting this morning."

Twenty minutes later we were in the car driving back to the Summit. Today I was dressed in a sleek black sheath dress with shiny black shoes. I couldn't help but feel a little bit like Audrey Hepburn, and the fact that the soles of my heels were red made me feel even classier. Who would have thought wearing such expensive clothes would make me feel different? Not in an arrogant kind of way, but with my confidence. Most of the time, I wore baggy clothes, putting comfort first, but I'd never experienced this feeling of satisfaction as I did now.

Derrial was dressed to intimidate today. He wore a dark suit with a shiny black shirt underneath and no tie. As we approached the venue of the Summit, the softness in his features faded, replaced by a man who looked ready to rule the universe. My stomach tightened, and the car seemed to close in around me almost as if a menacing, black cloud had descended. Maybe it was the Vepar's version of a "game face" but his serious expression was extremely intimidating even though I had watched the change happen.

Derrial didn't say a word as we strolled into the enormous building. Guards stood everywhere, along with paparazzi.

Inside, Vepar and humans stood clumped in groups, but everyone seemed to take a collective breath as we entered the room. Derrial didn't stop to say hello to anyone, instead he strode in the room where the meeting was to be held, not looking back to see if I followed.

I found myself wanting to watch his face during this meeting, so I sat in a chair across the room from his designated table. He shot me a quizzical glance but said nothing about my move.

Only a few minutes passed, and the room filled. An air of expectancy flooded the space with everyone intently watching Derrial, expecting, waiting. After a few more minutes of him looking over some papers as if he didn't have the eyes of the whole world on him, he stood.

"As you know one of our main initiatives since coming to this planet has been to improve the quality of women's lives. On our planet, females are revered, they are worshipped. One of the first things we noticed about your planet during our first visits was the utter lack of care that is given to women on this planet. That's why we mandated the use of a new birth control and that's why we instituted higher penalties for crimes against women. Whether Earth wants it or not, things are going to improve. That's why today we'll be announcing a new mandate. All women will now submit to new health screenings, to be conducted every six months. Any medical concerns discovered will be automatically addressed at the cost of governments of each respective country represented at this Summit."

Silence.

Not a word.

Then as if someone had unleashed a typhoon, a rising sound of gasps and groans escalated, followed by loud whispers because this was huge. It was fucking goliath in terms of the impact it would have on our society.

Holy shit!

Derrial was forcing governments to cover medical bills for females! Who the hell was he again to sway such power?

I stared at him in shock. All of this came from a creature that literally had stalked me for a week and abducted me in the middle of the night. And now he claimed that women were important to him? Had I misread his intentions? Where I called it kidnapping, did he call it protection on his planet?

I studied the faces around the room. Shocked expressions, a few women nodding, and some men scowling.

But I didn't miss how Derrial's eyes focused on me for the entire speech. Even in a room full of people and the distance between us, I thrummed with a feeling deep in my gut for him. There was no way for me to escape his pure magnetism, for me not to want him. Not after he'd just showed part of his plan, and it wasn't horrific or the end of the world stuff. But simple things, like ensuring all females received the medical treatment they deserved for thousands who couldn't afford it. So many were too afraid to visit a doctor. This would change so many lives.

When I met Derrial's gaze, the sparkle in his blue eyes glinted, my knees weakened and damn him on how he affected me, how he touched me so deeply with his mandate. I wanted to keep hating him because I understood those emotions. The itch I felt for him now made me see him in a different light, but underneath the surface I couldn't forget what he was... Along with why he was so protective of human females.

I sensed his stare over me like a lover's caress. Maybe if I itched this persistent scratch, we'd both move on from one another. Maybe that was the answer right there to finally end his obsession with me. And mine with him.

WE WERE on our way back to the hotel from yet another dull cocktail event that night, and I was glad for it, as I'd had enough of watching the most attractive women on Earth paw at Derrial all night, trying to get his attention. For some reason it had bothered me. I scanned the traffic quietly as it passed by, trying to understand why I felt this way.

"The traffic. I never appreciated it before tonight." Derrial moved closer to me, taking my face in his free hand. Derrial's other hand softly stroked the skin that was showing from my short cocktail dress. "This skin has been torturing me," he murmured. My breathing shifted to panting as he slid a finger along the hem of my dress. He began to lift the hem higher, ignoring my startled gasp at the fact that he was doing that in the backseat of a car with a driver in the seat in front of us.

He brought my face closer to him but stopped short of kissing me. Instead, he lingered for a moment, and I breathed him in, losing myself momentarily to his touch, his scent, his nearness. When he finally crushed his lips to mine, my hand flew up and caught his, shocking both of us as I held him to me, greedy for the taste of him. As he kissed me, Derrial's hands urged my legs apart and he slipped his hand up so high that his fingers brushed against the silk of my underwear. I wrenched myself away from him, gasping for air. When his fingers moved to pull my underwear to the side, I locked my legs on his hand.

"No," I mouthed to him.

I could see the driver struggling to keep his eyes on the road as it was impossible for him to miss what was going on in the backseat.

Derrial took pity on me and withdrew his hand, giving me a smirk as he did so.

"I can smell you," he said, inhaling deeply and closing his eyes as if he was in ecstasy and the car was somehow full of my scent. I blushed and turned so I was staring out at the traffic and the historic buildings instead of looking at him. My lips burned from his efforts and it was a struggle to sit still in the car as we made our way to the hotel. I could see him in the reflection of my window, silently watching me with that infuriating look he always had that told me he could see right through me.

We couldn't get to the hotel fast enough.

By the time we had made our way to the Mandarin Oriental, I had almost convinced myself to go through with it. Sex with Derrial. It was clearly what he wanted. And maybe once the whole mystique of what having sex would be like with me was over, he would be over me and I would be left alone.

I ignored the part of me that balked at the idea of him leaving me alone.

He seemed in no hurry as we got out of the car. All of his motions were smooth...and slow. It took him what felt like a year to come and open my door, and then he chatted with the driver for another five minutes before we moved to go inside. The only thing that signaled that he still wanted me was his hand placement on the small of my back. It burned through my dress and into my skin and I was halfway certain that there would be an imprint in my skin when I took my dress off.

We walked slowly through the hotel lobby, Derrial stopping to chat with other Vepar staying there as we did so. They stared at me curiously, but Derrial never introduced me. Which was probably a good thing since his hand that was on my back had started to slowly trail lower, rendering me speechless.

We finally made it to the elevator, and he continued my torture by taking out and typing on the little silver device that I had seen him playing with occasionally.

"Is that a cell phone?" I asked, wanting to break the silence. He looked up at me, a slow grin on his face. "It's a computer," he said. "I'm going over the recordings from today so I can look more closely at who was in the audience and what their reaction was to it. It will help me know better what leaders we have to lean on, or what Vepar are thinking of going against my plans."

I looked at him shocked.

"How did it record all of that? Wasn't it in your pocket the whole time?"

He looked at me with what resembled an almost pitying expression. "We're watching you all the time, surely your news media told you that?"

I looked at him baffled; my thoughts momentarily sidetracked by what he had just told me. The elevator made it to our floor at that moment, the bell ringing to signal we were at our destination. We walked down the hallway to our suite, a million questions running around my mind. All of the questions disappeared when the doors opened.

Evidently Derrial had the same thing in mind as I did this evening.

The room was dimly lit with candles flickering in the breeze coming in from the open balcony doors. There were two bottles of Crystal in an ice bucket on the grand piano along with two flutes. Soft classical music was streaming in from the sound system that was wired throughout the suite. It was the most romantic setting that I had ever seen.

And the exact opposite mood I was trying to set. One and done was my goal tonight and I didn't need to be distracted by whatever he was trying to create here. Yes, he and his friends were the most gorgeous creatures I had ever seen. But if he thought I could forget that they were aliens who had taken over the world and ruined my life, he had another thing coming.

I blew out the candles as I passed by them. I could see him frown as I did so.

His hand flew out and caught my arm, pulling me against him roughly. "Kitten, did I read you wrong and you aren't the romantic type?" He asked in a raspy voice as he trailed his lips down my throat. He bit down softly, and I stiffened, remembering the other day and his reaction to my blood.

I pulled away from him, taking a few steps away so I could keep my wits about me. I would need them if I was going to keep control of the situation. Facing him, I slowly unzipped the side of my dress, sliding the dress off so that it pooled at my feet.

At first, Derrial's eyes widened, and I could see him thinking as he tried to understand my sudden willingness to play. He quickly recovered however and flashed me a wicked smile, walking up to me and tracing my lips with his fingers. The move sent shivers down my spine.

"I've thought about your lips all day. I've pictured you on your knees with that pretty little mouth wrapped around me sucking me off," he said, a growl rumbling in his throat as he spoke.

I melted at his words, desire pooling low in my stomach. The sensible side of me held on though. "What are you waiting for?" I asked, trying to give him the same smirk he always gave me.

His finger dropped from my face, trailing along my collarbone and leaving a trail of fire in its wake. "Your body was meant to be mine," he murmured, his eyes beginning to glow as he took another deep breath that looked like he was smelling me. Maybe that was a Vepar thing. "Has anyone ever told you that you had a body that was made to be fucked," he said, continuing his slow trail down my body.

I was standing in nothing but a strapless bra and thong and despite my best efforts he was beginning to cast a spell of seduction on me that I wasn't sure I could control. I shook my head at his question, thinking about the trail of boyfriends I had left that had all been terrible to boring in bed.

"It is. In fact, I've never seen something I wanted so much before," he continued. I couldn't force a reply out of my mouth. I couldn't think clearly with his hand touching me like that.

"I need to taste you, kitten. It's all I've been thinking about for days. Will you let me do that?"

I moaned a yes. Derrial didn't wait for more encouragement. His fingers caught the waistband of my thong and ripped them away. He dropped to his knees and urged my legs apart.

"Wider," he ordered, and I shocked us both by immediately widening my stance. "Perfect." His hands moved along my thighs and when he reached his destination, he spread it wide and studied it for a moment, a look of appreciation on his face, before his fingers found my cleft. My eyes snapped back shut as he pushed two fingers inside of me.

"Are you always this wet?" he asked.

I shook my head again. "Do I do this to you?" he asked, fucking me slowly with his fingers. I nodded. "Say it, kitten."

"Yes."

"Yes, what? What do I do to you?"

"You make me wet," I moaned.

"Good girl," he murmured with approval. He continued to tease me with his fingers for a few seconds and then the warm rasp of his tongue sent a series of shivers trembling through my body. He licked across me leisurely as his fingers continued to plunge into me. I began to shake as I neared the edge. He pulled away; the effect similar to being doused with ice.

"Not until I say, kitten."

I whimpered at the command, but it gave me the resolve I needed to try and take back control. I didn't need to enjoy tonight, I just needed to get through it. Taking his hand, I pulled him towards one of the bedrooms. I could feel his frustration trailing behind me as we walked.

Despite the fact that his ministrations thus far had lit my entire body on fire, I aimed for a look of nonchalance as I crawled across the bed and laid down on my back looking at him.

I was acutely aware of his eyes on my naked skin as I laid there, but I pretended to ignore the effect he had on me. If he didn't think I liked it, he wouldn't want it again, right? No one wanted a disinterested lover. I was just hopeful that my momentary lapses where he was concerned would be forgotten if the overall package was disappointing.

Derrial slowly took off his jacket and undid his tie. It was amazing that after everything that had happened already this evening that he could still look perfect. He undid his shirt, showcasing a perfect tapestry of golden skin that defied all logic. I had somehow forgotten how good he looked without a shirt over the past few days. He was unreal.

I wondered again if this was his real form or if the Vepar could somehow change their forms to look pleasing to the human eye. If that was the case, he had nailed it. My thoughts flickered over to thinking of what Thane and Corran looked like without a shirt, but Derrial quickly got my attention back by unbuttoning the top of his dress pants and pulling out the most impressive cock I had ever seen. He began to stroke it while looking at me through a hooded gaze. I couldn't keep my eyes off of it. If they did change their appearances, he had gone a little too big. He must have seen my look of panic because he chuckled darkly and took a few steps closer to the bed until he was standing right on the edge of it.

"Don't worry, kitten. It will fit," he said.

"Spread your legs," he ordered, and somehow, I found myself dropping my legs open as he finished dropping his pants so that he was completely naked standing in front of me. He started to crawl across the king bed towards me, so blatantly seductive that I could feel myself becoming wetter just by watching him.

He moved on top of me, hovering there with those strange glowing eyes staring at me as if he was looking for something in my eyes. I gulped. This was actually happening. "Aren't you forgetting a condom?" I asked, suddenly thinking of getting a strange alien disease or worse, a strange alien baby. They had us on mandatory birth control, but I had never seen a discussion if it worked on the Vepar.

Something flickered in his eyes again, but it was gone before I could tell what it was. "Your birth control protects against pregnancy by any species. It's infallible unlike the birth control your human doctors were giving you before. As for diseases, it's impossible for us to carry diseases as our bodies have evolved past that. You'll probably be healthier after this," he said wryly.

I hesitated, not sure if this was a trick. What would he have to gain by getting his hapless human prisoner pregnant? Surely that would be the last thing he wanted. "Ok," I told him, hesitantly.

His eyes glowed up even more before he suddenly struck, sheathing himself inside of me at the same time as he bit into my neck, causing me to cry out as a wave of euphoria like nothing I had experienced before passed over me. I came immediately, tightening around him in what already felt like a vice grip.

He drove into me in relentless strokes, moving to my mouth after his initial taste of my blood. I could feel it running down from my wound. I could taste the coppery flavor as he attacked my lips.

I found myself crying his name as another orgasm splintered through me in violent waves. He continued his thrusts as he raced towards his own, not taking his eyes from me as he did so. There was blood all over his face. He looked more heathen than man in that moment, his eyes glowing so brightly that it almost hurt to look at them.

The moment felt too intimate and I turned my head away from him. "No," he growled, in a voice that was so dark and deep that I didn't recognize it in the moment. My gaze flew back to his. It was as if something inside of him had taken over and it was no longer Derrial in the body above me.

His hands clenched my hips tightly, and I was sure there would be marks there in the morning. He continued to thrust until I could tell the moment that he came undone. Just as I felt him tighten inside of me, he reared back and struck at my neck again. This time the pleasure was so powerful that I passed out, the last thing I saw were those glowing eyes of his looking at me possessively. Everything was dark after that.

10

*W*hen I woke the next morning, my body felt like I did right before the flu hit; achy and feverish. I laid in bed for a moment with my eyes closed, getting my bearings, wondering how a sickness could have struck so quick when I'd been feeling fine before. I shifted and an ache bit between my legs and on my neck. Instantly, I sat up with a start, my eyes flying open as I remembered what happened last night. I scanned the room for Derrial, but I was alone. He'd gone and left me here? We'd scratched our insatiable itch, so was I now free? I ignored the part of my heart that flickered with what felt like pain at the thought.

This was what I had hoped for, so now I could go home. Thinking of my hovel of a loft and my job that gave me just enough for bare essentials and not anything else didn't fill me with the happiness it had in the past. But it was still freedom in a way.

No sooner had those thoughts passed through my mind then the front door of the suite opened with a click, and a second later Derrial came into view. I tugged the blanket up to my neck, suddenly very much aware of the fact I remained naked. Of course, I shouldn't have been shy or had my cheeks on fire after our time together last night, but in truth, those memories of letting myself go made the embarrassment worse. I'd wanted him like I needed air, and just remembering our time together sent a shiver of excitement down through me.

He looked somehow brighter this morning, a huge smile on his face, the corners of his eyes crinkling. He seemed to carry a vibrant sexiness this morning. Plus, his skin seemed to have a sun-kissed glow. He wore a perfect suit as usual, today's was a black pinstripe one with a light blue shirt underneath. In a word, I couldn't believe I slept with a specimen that looked that perfect. An alien who for years I'd detested. Now, my emotions left me lost and confused.

I glanced at myself in the mirror hanging on the side wall and saw how tired I looked, dark circles under my eyes, and my hair sat limp, in desperate need of a wash. My skin appeared abnormally pale. I glanced back at Derrial who stared at me with a speculative gaze. I tried to remember if I'd ever heard of health repercussions for humans who had sex with Vepar, but all I could think of were the stories I'd read about women, and men, who became addicted to whatever the Vepar did in bed. How they spent every moment trying to get the Vepar to notice them and "keep" them. Those people had become obsessive, and I prayed that didn't happen to me, especially with the way I admired Derrial.

So, if the Vepar weren't hazardous to your health, then why did I look and feel like an extra in the Night from the Living Dead?

"How are you feeling this morning, kitten?" Derrial asked in a nonchalant tone.

I scowled at him, now even more suspicious. "What did you do to me?" I asked, my body shaking from the flu like symptoms that seemed to be growing worse. "

"You mean besides the best sex of your life?" he stated in that same casual tone that was beginning to drive me crazy as my anxiety escalated.

I gestured between the two of us with a flick of my hand. "Why do you look like you just got off a yearlong vacation whereas I look and feel like I'm hovering on death's door?"

He stared at his nails as if there was something on them before answering. "Oh, are you feeling the effect of the incomplete bond? I've heard that can be painful to experience," he explained nonchalantly as if we were discussing the latest score of the Lakers.

Bond.

What the fuck.

My heart slammed into my ribcage. What was he talking about? Granted I hadn't done my best to learn as much about the Vepar after my parents vanished as I could, but I'd think if there was such a thing as bonding between humans and Vepar, surely someone would have mentioned it by now?

"What do you mean? What bond?" I whispered in a hoarse voice, curling forward as I clutched the blanket to my chest tighter.

"I'm sure you remember my bites from last night?" he asked with a smirk as if proud of himself. "The bite is something that dates back to Vepar ancestors, it was a way to claim property...or claim their mate. It made it so that the intended creature was bound to males because of the enzymes that are deposited in their skin. The symptoms you're feeling are withdrawal symptoms. They'll only be evened out by either me biting you again...or you drinking my blood."

I stared at him in shock, fury rising inside of me so hot and thick that it might as well be burning me alive. It must have only been a few hours since he'd bitten me for the second time. How often did I need him to sink his teeth into me in order to stave off these symptoms? Symptoms that grew worse as the minutes ticked by, to the point that if I stood, I was certain I'd collapse. And drink his blood? Was he out of his mind? I wasn't a vampire. Just the thought had bile hitting the back of my throat.

"I have to leave in just a few minutes for the Summit, kitten. What's it going to be? Take a small sip of blood and be fine, or let me take a bite?"

My stomach turned at both options even as I remembered how my body buzzed, how aroused I grew from his attention last night.

Thinking about it, the bite felt more intimate than I was willing to admit this morning. And he'd said just a "sip of blood," which couldn't be that bad, right? Hell, was I really contemplating this? I had a feeling that I was going to regret this, but what was the alternative? Keep feeling like I'd been run over by a truck, which then backed up over me, again and again.

"I don't want to bite you, so you'll have to cut yourself," I told him. Something like triumph flashed in his eyes, and I immediately wondered if I was about to make a horrible mistake.

He already pulled out a pocket knife from his pocket and slashed his hand before I could think further about it. "Hurry," he said. "This will heal quickly as my blood coagulates fast, and I'm not going to offer you this chance again." I gaped at the blood puddling on his hand. It wasn't red like mine but carried a bluish-green hue. Yet another reminder of who stood in front of me - a perfect being who wasn't human.

"Kitten," he growled, a thread of urgency in his voice as the wound started to close up in front of my eyes. Not allowing myself a chance to think anymore, I pulled his hand towards me, closed my eyes, and pressed the wound to my mouth. I took a slurp.

It was sweet, nothing like the salty tang of human blood. It wasn't an unpleasant taste at all, but the second I swallowed a tingling started to spread throughout my body just from the one small mouthful I'd taken. I broke away, pushed his hand from my mouth, and glared at him accusingly.

"Was that enough? Is it supposed to tingle like this?" I asked, gasping as a warm heat started to follow the tingles.

Derrial grinned, more satisfied than I'd ever seen him look. "The bond is forming. You should be back to your normal self soon," he said. He leaned closer and stroked my face softly, a expression on his face that was new, soft and tender. "I'll be back as soon as I can," he said before brushing a kiss across my lips, then he turned to stalk out of the door in that fluid, graceful way that all the Vepar had.

"I hate you," I threw after him.

He turned to look at me. "You know this is forever, right?" he asked with a sardonic smile appearing on his face even as I plotted a million ways to escape from this hell I'd found myself in.

He left the room, and I stared after him flabbergasted as the front door closed, signaling he'd left the suite. Still drowning in the tingling and warmth encasing my body, I wanted nothing more than to forget I'd just drank alien blood. What had I been thinking?

One thing was for sure. After taking his strange blood, I better wake up feeling like a brand-new woman, full of energy, or I was kicking someone's ass.

I curled up on my side and fell into a fitful sleep haunted by images of me sprouting horns and a tail and drinking the blood of hapless humans I came across.

BY THE TIME I woke up, I laid spread out on the bed, the bedsheets tangled around my legs, but I was breathing easy. I didn't know if it was the glorious sunlight drenching me in warmth from the window, or that I fell asleep so heavily, or the blood I'd taken from Derrial, but regardless, right now I felt incredible. So much so, I could swear I'd fly if I headed outside.

I stared out at the beautiful blue sky outside of the floor to ceiling windows deciding I loved living so high up in the air, sharing my space with birds and clouds. Was this what it would be like traveling in a spaceship when the Vepar came to Earth, keeping only the universe view for company? I'd heard on TV a Vepar once saying, the crew slept for most of the trip, so maybe it wouldn't be so great. Plus, the one time I did catch a flight as a child, I got the worst motion sickness.

I realized that I was rambling to myself and tried to slow down my thoughts, but for the first time in too long, a newfound joy beamed through me, and I couldn't even understand the reason.

My stomach growled with hunger, and with no idea how long I'd been asleep, I untangled myself from the sheets and pushed my legs over to the edge of the mattress. I expected to hurt because earlier I wasn't sure that I would be able to walk without falling over, but as I climbed onto my feet, I bounced on my toes, feeling ready to run a marathon.

Damn, whatever had been in Derrial's blood had left me feeling amazing. At that moment my euphoria cleared enough that I was able to remember his words about our bond. A cold dread shifted over me, pushing out the strange joy I had just been feeling. I needed to find out what exactly the bond meant, knowing that I wasn't going to like whatever it meant. It was ridiculous for me to think that he could have at least told me about it first. After all, he hadn't exactly asked for my permission before kidnapping me from my world.

I padded over on bare feet into the kitchen admiring how the floorboards in this hotel were shiny and so clean. I pictured myself living somewhere like this, with such luxury, and I doubted I'd ever leave to go outside. Not when I had everything I needed right here.

Like the previous days, I swiftly scanned the tables and couches in case Derrial or one of the guards had left behind their cells considering all the phones had been removed from this penthouse. Maybe I was being foolish in even believing I had anyone to call for help. After witnessing Derrial's influence over world leaders, what exactly would authorities do if I called, insisting he'd kidnapped me? I wasn't a fool not to know how badly that could go for me. I would need a different tactic. Sure, I loved it here, but this was me floating high on an alien's blood and daydreaming of living in a fairytale.

Stomping over to the fridge, I pulled it open, expecting food, but instead I stared at bottles of water. I sighed before having a bright idea. I grabbed some water and headed over to the couch. I flopped down and collected the menu from the hotel's restaurant. This would all be under Derrial's name, which meant I could order anything.

Once I made my choice, I headed to the front door and cranked it open. In a flash, a guard stepped in my path, broad shouldered and enormous.

"You can't leave," he snorted.

"Fine by me." I shrugged and handed him a piece of paper.

He stared at it, his brow furrowing in a dozen lines, then glanced up at me quizzically without accepting the note.

I pushed it to his hand once again. "I'm hungry and I need you to go order this food for me."

He cocked an eyebrow, stiffening as if getting me food was below his pay rank. The other guard farther down the corridor chuckled, and I noted only two of them guarded my door.

I slouched a hip into the door frame and huffed. "Do you really want me to tell Derrial I've been starving all day, close to fainting, because you refused to get me a bit of food?"

He made a grunting sound deep in his chest, glaring at me from hooded eyes, and snatched the paper from my hand before studying it. He snorted. "A bit of food? Where are you going to put all this?" Looking my way, he scanned me head to toe. "And there's no salad or vegetable in sight?"

I gritted my teeth, refusing to show him how much I wanted to hit him in the nose, even if it required me to get on tippy toes to do so. If I was trapped in a penthouse, then I was spoiling myself, and right now I was so hungry, it made me impatient and my pulse raced with a desperation to eat something.

"Don't forget the sundae." I stepped back inside and slammed the door shut.

Where had my feistiness come from, all in the name of

food? Hell hath no fury when my stomach rumbled. I smirked, grabbed an apple from the complimentary hotel fruit basket, and crashed onto my bed while switching on the television.

Half an hour later and still no food, I was about to check with the guards where my order was, when the click of the front door sounded.

Yes!

I hurried out of my bedroom, calling out over my shoulder, "Give me a sec, I'll be right out."

With my mouth already salivating and deciding I'd devour the sundae first, I rushed down the hallway and into the living room.

But instead of food waiting for me, I found Derrial, his back to me, staring out the window. He wore jeans and a black dress shirt. When did he get changed? Peering at him closer, I realized that he stood wrong. One shoulder sat slightly lower than the other, he looked somehow smaller, deflated. Strange since he was a man who towered over others, never backing down. Maybe something had happened at the Summit?

"Derrial? Is everything okay?"

He didn't respond at first, but he cracked his neck, and a shiver slithered up my back. Unease crept over me when he didn't answer.

"What's going on?" I asked.

The space around him seemed to quiver or was I seeing things?

When he started to turn around, the room dimmed...

Something was very wrong.

The energy around him darkened and now flowed off his body like waves. And when he faced me, I gasped.

My stomach sunk through me, rattling me at the core.

"Who are you?" I recoiled, hugging myself, noting he stood in my way to escape.

A different Vepar I'd never seen before stood before me, and in a heartbeat, he lunged towards me. Eyes wide and dark, hands reaching out for me.

I screamed when my world tilted under me.

11

When I woke up, darkness surrounded me. It took me a second to gain my bearings, but eventually I realized I was slouched in some kind of chair. It was a darkness like nothing I had ever experienced before. It was so thick I wouldn't have even been able to see my hands in front of my face even if they weren't bound behind my back. There wasn't even a beam of light coming in from under a door. It was a darkness like nothing I had experienced before. I went through the last things I could remember and the image of the unfamiliar Vepar crashed into my memory. The last thing I remember was looking into his eyes... Eyes that were completely black as if his pupil had taken over everything, and a pasty face as if he had no pulse. A shiver raced down my spine at the memory.

I was getting tired of being kidnapped. I'd take waking up in a mansion in a sunny room over this experience any day though. I tugged on the bindings on my wrist, trying to see if they would loosen at all, but they held firm.

"Hello," I called out, feeling like one of those girls in the horror movies right before their death.

I waited for a moment, but I couldn't hear anything. I opened my mouth to call out again when the strangest thing happened. It was like all the darkness was sucked out of the room in an instant and suddenly there were glowing brick walls all around, and the strange Vepar stood in front of me. I watched as the last remnants of darkness were sucked into him.

I had never seen anything like it.

The man wore the same black shirt and jeans Derrial had on when I first saw him. He slowly studied me before beginning to circle me. He stopped in front of me, and I watched, again amazed, as the blonde hair that he'd been using to impersonate Derrial melted away, leaving a Vepar with hair so dark that it matched his strange black eyes. I gasped. That was the most alien thing I'd seen so far.

Staying on the theme of horror movies, he looked like a character from one of those movies that portrayed people who were possessed by demons. Except I was pretty sure the creature standing in front of me was far scarier than a demon would be. For one, I'd seen enough flicks and read enough to know what a demon was. But this thing in front of me... I had zero clue and that terrified me. I shook in my chair, desperate to run. Except, I was stuck inside a room.

Another prison.

And this time I was with a monster.

"So fascinating," he whispered in a voice that was as smooth and slick as oil. The voice seemed to emanate from inside my brain, and I shook my head at the strange feeling.

I knew I shouldn't say something, but my curiosity won out. "What's fascinating?" I asked.

The creature grinned. Unlike the other Vepar I'd seen who all seemed to have perfect movie star smiles, this one carried a mouth filled with razor sharp teeth, kind of like a shark. I had been thinking that this creature was a Vepar, but now that I had seen the strange teeth, I wasn't so sure. All I knew was that this being made Derrial and the others look as friendly as a teddy bear compared to him.

"It's something I'm sure they weren't anticipating," the creature muttered to himself, still staring at me avidly. He must have seen the look of confusion on my pale face because he smiled again, flashing those horrid teeth that had me pressing back into my chair. "The bond, little human. You're the first successful human/Vepar bond to be completed since they started trying. And by completing the bond, you also became the target for every Vepar enemy in the vicinity." He chuckled and the sound was like knives down my arms.

Nope, nothing good would come from this thing in front of me.

I must have still been staring at him with a dumb look on my face because he continued. "Humans normally don't even appear on our radar. Your species are like ants scurrying about with no idea of anything that's going on around them. Only higher-level beings garner any interest." He raised his chin, his shoulders back.

He went on, "Vepar and all the rest are almost like glowing figures in night vision goggles, they're easy to spot. While they appear as a faint glow, you my dear are like the fireworks. You light up the darkness like nothing I've ever seen before. Every creature within a hundred galaxies will want you. And I got to you first." His voice darkened and he almost drooled at saying those last few words.

I was trying to absorb his words and their meaning. "If what you're saying is true, how did you get to me so fast. The bond only just happened."

He smiled again, his teeth sending sharp shivers of

dread throughout my body, and I decided right then I loathed his smile. Better he grimaced.

"We had something planned for the Summit. But when I saw you, everything changed. You were too good to pass up," he answered with a shrug.

"What are you?" I demanded.

The room started to darken, black mists erupted from his skin until it started to envelop everything, creating that same all-encompassing blackness as before.

"We are the Khonsu," his voice whispered, seeming to be coming from all around me. I could feel something stroking my face, almost like a hand. It was as if the dark mists were an extension of him.

Suddenly the faint touches changed from a soft sensation to what felt like a whip lashing across my face. A jolting pain shuddered across my cheek, and I screamed as the lashes spread all over my body, ripping at my skin.

I screamed and tucked my chin low, but my hands tied at my back kept me locked to the chair.

A piercing pain seared across my body worse than a branding iron.

It was impossible to tell where the next lash would hit next since I couldn't even see an inch from my face. All my mind could comprehend was pain. I lost all thoughts; all I could do was burrow my head into my chest. Away from the pain radiating me, burning me alive.

The assault never relented, never stopped, never gave me a chance.

Blood soaked my torn clothes, each new strike a sharp bite to my flesh, ripping me to shreds. My throat grew raw from cries, but they went unheard.

In those moments, I prayed for my death, to be taken because I couldn't take another second.

As if sensing my end, the whips paused, granting me a brief reprieve. Tears tracked my cheeks and fell over my jawline, every inch of me drowning with agony.

I glanced up from the curtain of my hair covering my face, looking for the creature, hoping for an end. But as before, only darkness surrounded me.

Still, I sensed the bastard. Felt him in my head because just when I would recover enough to stay conscious, the whips returned.

Over and over he tortured me, and his laughter echoed in my head.

Please god, kill me.

My whole life I'd fought for survival, battled through depression after losing my parents, struggled to keep a job and keep myself going every day for the simple reason that my mom and dad would have wanted me to, that one day I might see them again.

But now... Now I had enough of everything. The exhaustion tore through me, and I no longer wanted to face the shitstorm of my life. This was it.

Just like most things in my life, I was taken, forced, and shoved aside. And I went along each time, believing in hope. But I'd been fooling myself, and now I had enough. I needed the exit button because I wanted to tap out.

I hiccupped a strangled cry and ached as a deep strike raked down my back. I floated back and forth out of consciousness.

In that moment, I would have done anything to escape.

The agony faded once again, easing the darkness that was consuming me. I watched through barely open eyes as my tormenter appeared in front of me. He smirked and heaved each breath as if my bloody state and agony delighted him. But he looked different, gone was his pasty complexion, and now he carried a shiny, healthy glow like Derrial had earlier that morning. Was this creature somehow feeding on my blood too?

The fear in my veins melted under the inferno of rage drumming through me. I had enough of being used and abused by this monster.

As I slouched in the seat, my quickened breaths grew raspy during the small reprieve, and an idle thought floated through my mind. I'd been told of vampires around campfires as a little girl. And now meeting these aliens, I questioned if the tales didn't have it wrong. They romanticized vampires, others had them as misunderstood, or starved undead. But what if they were creatures who came from space to use humans? If I had known that as a little girl, I wouldn't have ever been able to sleep another wink.

"Such a strong, brave, little human," the creature cooed as he stepped closer. He reached out, catching a little of the blood that dripped from the side of my face. He licked the droplet he'd caught on his finger, almost sounding like he was having an orgasm when he tasted it, his eyes rolling back into his head, groaning. The sound disgusted me, bile climbing to my throat.

"You're beautiful painted in red," he declared, his eyes snapping open. Before he even started to let the darkness out once again, I was prepared for my life to end at that point, so nothing shocked me more than when the walls started to dissolve around us. The creature jerked around, his face twisting into a disfigured beast.

What was going on?

"I'll just take some for the road," he snarled, his upper lip creased with a look of disappointment. In haste, he swiped his palm across my bloody arm. I screamed in agony as white-hot pain raced over my skin as if his touch was barbed wire, shutting my eyes.

"See you shortly," he whispered in my ear and licked my neck, the sound turning my stomach.

When the pain had subsided enough for me to open my eyes, he was gone, and the walls had almost completely disintegrated with only a puff of dust in their place.

I couldn't imagine what creature was waiting for me now, I couldn't comprehend what could be scary enough to get the black-eyed devil to flee but whatever came next would end up killing me.

Shaking all over and my vision blurring in and out, I sat there with what felt like hundreds of open wounds, blood dripping on the concrete floor around the seat, and tried to prepare myself for death.

I was ready...Ready to face my maker. To end the horrendous pain.

Tears rolled down my face, stinging the cuts they fell into and continuing their journey down to the corner of my mouth. A hooded vale of death hung over me, and in that moment in time when I wasn't sure how I could ever recover, I welcomed the easy way out. As gutless as it sounded, I couldn't keep this up.

When a figure appeared where a wall had been minutes earlier, I blinked hard to clear my vision. Was I seeing right? A familiar, gorgeous, tatted Vepar appeared in front of me, my brain evidently having enough. I was hallucinating. Thane's penetrating gaze was the last thing that I saw before I finally let the effects of my wounds carry me away.

"Pet, wake up," were the words I woke to. I really would like to stop losing consciousness I decided as I struggled for what felt like the millionth time to open my eyes. I sighed as I felt a soft, wet cloth gently being moved over my burning wounds. The coolness helped ease away the pain somewhat but considering I felt as if I'd just climbed out of a pool it was clear that I was still bleeding profusely.

My muscles hurt as I tried to move them. When I finally wrenched my eyes open wide enough to see anything, I stared up into Thane's worried, blue gaze. I'm sure I looked like hell.

"Stay with me, pet," he murmured, continuing to move the cool cloth over my aching wounds. "We just need to get the bleeding to stop and you'll be better in a flash." He held a device similar to the one that corran had used on me at the mansion and started to run it over my injuries.

"Fuck."

His sudden outburst had me flinching, and I regretted the sudden movement as a searing pain shuddered through me.

He threw the device down beside him, his brow pinching, and he must have seen the questioning look in my eyes. "We use that device to heal skin lesions. That bastard must have used his darkness to inflict these wounds because I can't heal cuts this way."

It was like I could actually feel the life leaking out of my body. Thane had gently laid me down on the concrete floor in the torture room, and despite the ugliness of the location, I soaked up his beauty as he tended to my injuries. At least I'd have something gorgeous to look at as I died, I thought amusedly. There could be worse ways to die.

"So, we may have to do this the old-fashioned way." He offered me a soft smile and I wasn't sure if that was meant to be a joke.

"You could always take me to the hospital," I suggested in a whisper, well aware of what his answer would be, but figuring it was worth trying.

"That's not what I was talking about, pet." He brushed a strand of hair caught on my lashes out of my face. "The quickest way to remove your pain and heal you is with a blood exchange." He stared at me with a smirk as if he knew what Derrial and I had done.

"Do you mean a bond?" I asked, sounding snappier than I'd intended, or maybe I had meant it that way because no one had even explained what such a connection entailed. "You need to explain what a bond means first," I gasped even as a wave of pain shot up my leg and I convulsed as the pain rolled through me, faster and harder. Shutting my eyes, I let it pass and stayed statue still until the thrumming eased.

Soft fingers stroked my hand. "My blood will run in your veins and yours in mine. I will share with you some of my healing ability, but it also means..."

He wiped his mouth, almost nervous, and I looked at him, sensing something big was coming. "It means what?"

"The fact you didn't die when you were bound with Derrial means your blood is compatible with ours, and we were right to sense there was something special about you."

"What does..." My words trailed off from the burning pain, feeling as if someone jammed blades into my open injuries. "Why does it hurt so much?" I cried out, gripping Thane's hand, squeezing it as the deadening sensation crashed through me over and over.

His breath was on my cheek. "Pet, I can help you, but you have to willingly agree to bond with me. The darkness he used to cut you up has a toxin in it, made to bring you unbearable pain for weeks after the infliction."

Sweat slid down the side of my face, or maybe it was blood. I had no clue. I still stared at Thane incredulous though. Was he fucking kidding? He was staring at me with compassion and he had offered me a way out. Earlier I was willing to die to stop the torture, and now I was ready to be set free from the pain.

"Yes," I cried. "Please, make it stop."

"I will," was all he said, then took out a small blade from his belt. "I need to make a small incisor on fresh skin as your cuts have poison that sits on the wound."

"Do it. Hurry," I cried as another stream of pain rushed over me, making me feel like someone was raking nails across my body. The pain was so bad that I couldn't even tell Thane had finished cutting me until I glanced over and saw him pressing my finger into his mouth. His eyelids fluttered as if the taste did something to him, taking him to another realm.

When he finally lowered my hand and licked his bloody teeth, he sliced his thumb and pressed it to my parted lips. Drops rushed over my tongue, and I lapped the blood, its coppery, sweet taste flooding my mouth. Already, the sharpness of my wounds was retreating.

He must have cut himself deep, because I was taking in more than I had with Derrial. As my pain eased, I gripped his hand, holding on. I needed more until the pain was completely stopped. As I drank his blood, I found myself forgetting the day, forgetting that I had ever been hurt.

Thane ripped his hand from my grip, his thumb tugged out of my mouth, making a popping sound.

I licked my lips feverishly, in those seconds believing he might try to take the blood back.

"Enough," he growled. "Blood sharing can become an addiction, so we need to be careful."

As I lay there, feeling the calmness spread over me, I remembered the monster's words. How I shone so bright they'd find me, how I was special, and how his kind, the Khonsu, would hunt me down. A different fear strangled me now, and it became hard to breathe once again as the truth of my reality slammed into me.

No matter where I ran or hid, I'd never be safe.

12

"Who are the Khonsu?" I shuffled in my bed in the mansion, pulling the blanket to my chest. Thane had flown us both back to their place in the helicopter after exchanging blood with me. Derrian needed to attend an urgent matter in another country so he hadn't returned home yet after he had been assured by Thane that I was safe. I suspected Derrian was an ambassador for his home planet, even though he had refused to tell me what his position was while I was with him. But it would explain why he seemed to be so damn important. I wished he would hurry home so that I could ask him more questions. Despite how my relationship had changed with the Vepar, I still wanted to know all about them and how the hell I could avoid them and the Khonsu for eternity.

"You need to get some sleep for the blood to fully heal you," Thane insisted, staring down at me, his strong arms folded over his chest. I couldn't help but stare at where his biceps bulged. With his short, dark hair, he could easily pass for a god. He looked like he was almost built of stone, and ready to battle any monster.

I lifted my arm and wiggled it. My wounds had healed to thin marks on my skin. "Looks pretty good to me. Your blood is like magic. You could help so many humans with it, you know."

He studied me, and I wasn't sure if he intended to burst out laughing or scold me. "My blood is toxic to anyone who isn't compatible with our kind."

There was that word again. *Compatible.* The way he said it made it sound so robotic. But why was I special to the Vepar? I gained healing from them, but what did they get from me? I tried not to think too hard about the fact that Derrial took the chance to exchange our blood, knowing if I wasn't compatible, I'd die. We would be talking about that later. I'm just glad their hunch that I was "special" from the beginning had been true.

"Khonsu," he began, and I shoved all other thoughts aside, focused on his words. "They're a race that inhabit my home planet, Veon." He paused for a moment, the wheels of thinking spinning behind his gaze. He sat on the bed's edge, facing me. "I'll try to explain using Earth terms. There are over 400 billion stars in the Milky Way, and all kinds of races exist there. But Veon circles a sun that is the closest to your Solar System. Your scientists call it Proxima Centauri."

I nodded, wishing I had my phone to Google all of this. I tried to lock it in my memory for later.

"The Khonsu aren't originally from Veon. They arrived after the sun near their home planet died. They apparently came from one of the rings of stars that circled the Milky Way. Their kind had to either escape or die, and we accepted them onto our land."

I nodded, wondering if there was more to these Khonsu then what had first appeared. I couldn't imagine what it would have been like to get up one morning and leave a planet forever.

"At first, they settled on the isolated side of Veon, but soon, Vepar started going missing, and we later discovered the Khonsu were hunting our kind, killing us in masses, to take the planet for themselves. We also found out we weren't the first race to have them attack in this manner. And now we hunt one another on Veon, and it's unsafe for anyone."

Engrossed, I almost forgot to breathe. "Holy shit! So, what the hell are they doing on Earth?"

He exhaled loudly, his shoulders sagging forward. "Some stowed away on our ships when we came to Earth."

I recalled Derrial's threat about the dog-like creatures escaping from the vessel. I still didn't know if those creatures were real, but the creature that I knew for sure had escaped was a million times scarier.

"You should get some sleep now." He pulled the blanket to my chin, but I didn't want to sleep. I had so many questions, so many things I had to understand.

As he turned to leave, I grabbed his wrist. "Please, don't leave."

He stared at our connection, at my hand so pale and small against his tanned skin, his strong arm. When he met my eyes, an expression I didn't understand fluttered across his face, and his breathing quickened. His reaction made my pulse start to race as the heat from where our skin touched spread over to me.

I released my hold, and he sank onto the edge of the bed, pulling a bent leg between us as he faced me.

"Nothing will harm you in this home. It's reinforced, and you're safe."

"Why did the Khonsu come after me?"

With a deep inhale, he sighed. "We never should have let you go to the Summit, but we didn't know the Khonsu had infiltrated the meeting. Or maybe they didn't infiltrate it, and they just happened to see you while you were outside."

I swallowed hard. "That doesn't answer my question."

"Just like we sensed there was something different about you, so can they."

"Is that why you brought me to your house in the first place? That Khonsu said I glowed and that I was easy to detect to your kind."

The corners of his mouth tightened. "He's not our kind," he snapped, then inhaled sharply. "We are different races, but share some abilities, like blood bonding. For us, it's about finding our forever mate, but for them, it's a feeding frenzy as others' blood heightens their energy. It makes them stronger, feeds their adrenaline, and not even one of your human bullets would stop them. They have one purpose. Take over worlds and hunt down as many compatible females to feed from."

"Crap." I paused for a moment. "Wait! Why wouldn't they attack men for their blood?" I pulled my knees up under the blanket and hugged them.

"Only females carry the pheromone."

I swallowed the boulder in my throat because this told me the women on their planet were in danger, and the men would have had to step up to protect them, save them.

"What's stopping them from going out there and finding another compatible woman to drink their blood?"

"You're the only one we've found so far on Earth, and we've been watching your planet for years."

I studied him for a long pause. "So, you came to search for compatible females?"

He paused and the way the features on his face morphed

into an expressionless one, I suspected there were more reasons for their interest in Earth, and not something he'd just offer up.

"You're special, Ella," he said.

I choked on a forced laugh. "If being special means attracting the attention of a blood-sucking monster, then count me out. I don't want any of this."

He looked at me with pity in his gaze, but that wouldn't help me. What was I going to do? Hide out in this mansion forever?

"How do I stop them from coming after me?" I pleaded, my voice coming out barely a whisper.

This time, he took my hand in his. "If we knew that answer, we would have eradicated them from our planet long ago."

His confession sat in my gut like concrete, spreading, dragging me into a sea of fear because it meant I was stuck. These things that snuck onto Earth now saw me as a means to make themselves stronger, and I wasn't a fool to ignore what that entailed.

Me imprisoned.

For life.

Tortured and whipped.

Drained of blood but kept alive so they could keep taking and taking.

I could barely take a breath as I pictured myself locked up for life by these things.

Thane's thumb caressed the back of my hand in small circles. The move was slow and tender, and it made me glance over at him. He must have seen the fright on my face because he leaned closer, his arms reaching out and looping around my back. He pulled me against him. Embraced by his strength, I let myself melt against the rock wall that was his chest, my ear just above his heart.

Bang. Bang. Bang. It thumped.

"We'll be by your side always."

But my mind refused to make sense of his words because all I heard was forever, and that terrified me. How could they stay with me so long? And then they mentioned the whole being bonded to me forever. What the hell did that mean? Forever until I died of old age? I couldn't live a life without freedom, without the chance to make more friends, to maybe even get married and have kids. Not that I wanted that now but wasn't that what people did? Maybe that wasn't possible in our world now with the Vepar here.

On one bright side, if the Khonsu couldn't find another compatible person, they wouldn't have to kill anyone. Maybe they'd leave this planet, or perhaps the Vepar had already put into motion a means to eradicate them from our planet. I didn't know the answer to anything, I just wanted to survive. To not be miserable, or be dragged down with fear, and definitely to not be tortured.

This was a new world we all had ventured into and the unknown was like an ominous cloud over all our heads.

Were the Vepar really here as a potential backup home in case they couldn't remove the Khonsu on their planet or before all their females were killed by the Khonsu? But then why would they bother bonding to me? Or did I have it all wrong and they bonded to many females, which begged the question of what they got out of the connection? Dozens of questions circled my mind, my head buzzed, and didn't want to face any of this because things seemed so much more complicated than I anticipated.

Thane rubbed my back, his breath washing through my hair, his arms were like lifebelts wrapped around me.

"Will I ever have my normal life back?" I finally broke the silence and glanced up.

He stared down at me, his blue eyes glinting. "You will always be safe with us," he said again.

I couldn't find any words to say to him as he had basically just admitted I would never be returning home. I pressed my cheek back against his chest, seeking comfort even though he was partially the cause of all my problems. The dreaded answer I knew all along was now confirmed. Normality was gone for me, and only uncertainty lay ahead. While so many other questions poured through my mind about where I'd live such an existence, and if they intended to stay on Earth forever, I didn't ask them. I couldn't bear to hear the answers because holding myself together now was hard enough as I trembled in his arms and tears pricked my eyes.

Everything I knew would change.

Any dreams I had were gone forever.

I curled further into Thane.

He nudged me slightly as he shuffled further onto the bed and climbed in under the blanket with me. Taking me into his arms once again, we lay together, tears sliding out of the corners of my eyes. Everything was happening so fast, and now I couldn't even be angry at the three Vepar. If they found me glowing, then the Khonsu would have done so sooner or later and I would much rather be with the Vepar than the Khonsu.

"Everything will be alright," Thane whispered softly, his voice as light as a caress. He kissed the top of my head and I couldn't help the warmth that spread over me.

I'd be lost without their protection, because nothing would ever be all right again. Not a single thing.

I woke with a start, my pulse jumping beneath my skin, my heart banging in my ears. A droplet of sweat rolled down the side of my face, while the room spun around me. I could have sworn I had just experienced the worst nightmare of my life, but somehow, I couldn't remember a single thing that had happened in the dream. Only the darkness lingered in my chest, that ominous feeling that told me danger lay near.

When I pushed myself up in bed, I shuddered at the sight in front of me.

This *was* my bedroom in the mansion, except it wasn't. Instead of the walls and ceiling, lofty trees crowded together, grand ones with busy branches covered in the greenest leaves. They swayed and the rustling flooded the room, yet I felt no wind.

What the hell was going on? I rubbed my eyes, but the trees remained.

In slow motion, I crept out of bed, almost tripping from the sheets tangled around my legs. Tugging on the blanket, I finally freed myself and stumbled, teetering on my feet and falling against a tree.

I glanced up into the canopy covering the ceiling. Everything seemed so real, but I didn't understand how it could be. I felt a nearby tree and pulled back immediately in surprise. The bark was rough and bumpy under my hand.

A fogginess clung to my mind as I tried to think straight, work out what exactly was going on. From across the bedroom, a shadow shifted in the far corner, and my heart hit the back of my throat. Sliding across the wall of trees behind me, a scream pushed through my lungs as the darkness flitted across the opposite wall as if mimicking my actions.

Was this some kind of Vepar thing, or had the Khonsu found me? Thane said I'd be safe here, that the mansion was protected. But then where the freak did the trees come from? My head felt like it was swimming in fog.

I reached for the door handle and opened it in slow motion. Barely able to breath, I turned and sprinted out of the bedroom.

The hallway blurred around me, everything fuzzy and jumpy, but I didn't care. Not when dread crept up the back of my legs and there was a monster in the house.

More trees flanked the passage as I ran faster than possible toward the stairs.

A quick glance back, and the shadow emerged, a lofty figure with piercing red eyes.

My earlier scream tore past my throat, and I darted down the steps, moving too fast. Everything felt strange, like I was moving in slow motion and I couldn't run faster. It was going to catch me, just like the Khonsu. And I doubted I'd survive this time.

A thundering sounded around me, getting louder, closer.

Panic gripped me, and my feet tangled over one another. I tripped, the world racing up toward me. Everything was happening too fast, and my sight was blurring in and out.

Something huge raced up toward me from the kitchen. There were more of those creatures?

I cried out louder as I fell, my arms fluttering outward for something to grab onto.

I hit the ground; except I didn't hit the wooden floorboards like I was expecting. I landed in someone's arms, soft and strong at the same time. It had gotten me. I wasn't going to go down easily, so I started to kick and punch, digging my nails into whatever I could.

"Ella!" Thane's voice found me.

"Help," I shouted, thrashing, my vision still a wash of blurs and shapes.

Someone grasped my hands and legs, carrying me as if I were a sacrifice. Two figures hovered over me. I kept blinking, shaking my head to clear the fuzziness, the tears making it worse.

Finally, I was laid on something soft, the hands releasing me.

I scrambled backward into a corner, rubbing my eyes, and slowly the view in front of me cleared. It seemed to still be blurry, but as I stared up, I could see well enough to realize that Thane and corran were in front of me, both wearing worried expressions.

"There is something upstairs," I blurted frantically, pointing to the stairs.

Corran stared up, following my pointed finger, while Thane suddenly had a glass of liquid in his hand. He pushed it into my grasp.

"Drink."

I did. It had a sweet fruity flavor that I didn't recognize. But I was so thirsty that I gulped down the whole glass, drenching the heat consuming me. "Why are there trees upstairs? Is that some weird Vepar technology?"

They exchanged glances before looking down at me once more, Thane's mouth spreading into a grin.

"Pet, there are no trees upstairs, no monsters either. You're safe."

I stared at him for the longest moment, then glanced up

to see the branches of a tree sticking out from the hallway. Looking back at the men, I couldn't remember if I had responded to them. They were staring at me as if I'd lost my mind. We continued to stare at each other. I wasn't sure how much time was passing without words, but I couldn't seem to form any. It felt like fifteen minutes had passed, maybe more before I could finally find my voice. I said, "It's up there, go and see."

Running a hand over his face, Corran collected the empty glass from my grip while Thane headed upstairs, right past the trees without giving them a glance.

Was I imagining this? I kept shaking my head, unable to dislodge the feeling I was floating on air. Was I still dreaming? Staring at my hand, it seemed to shine. Wow, this was new.

"Ella?" Someone touched my hand and I looked down to find it was Thane, crouching in front of me.

When had he come back downstairs? "You're hallucinating, pet. It's a normal reaction from the poison on your wounds from the Khonsu."

I shook my head, and the room tilted around me. "Whoa, did you feel that?"

"You just need to sit here and let that drink get through your system." Corran flopped down next to me. He looped an arm around my back and brought me closer. I lay on my side, with my head on his lap. His hand stroked my hair so gently, it lulled me into a calmness, my raging pulse easing.

My eyelids closed and I let myself fall under his touch.

I had no idea how much time had passed, but when I opened my eyes, the sunlight had dimmed and now Thane shared the sofa with me. We were alone, and he looked down at me, caring for me, holding me tight. But something felt different inside of me, an emptiness and barren feeling I hadn't had before. I was lost in a world that was meant to be my home, or was it that I felt trapped?

"I think something's wrong," I murmured. "I feel wrong."

He smiled and pushed a lock of hair out of my face. "What can I do to aid you?" And with those words, a mischievous grin split his lips.

13

"Make me feel something, Thane. Please..." I begged, the words so easily falling from my lips. I was never needy, I hadn't ever been allowed to be. But right now, I longed to feel his touch. I needed to feel his skin on mine, to wrap my arms tightly around him, to feel him consume me. To feel he was real, that they all were real. To remind myself I wasn't all alone in the world even though it felt like it in that moment.

He scooped me up in his arms, carrying me to the room upstairs where I was glad to see there actually were no trees, setting me down on my feet beside the bed. He took my face in his hands, his beautiful blue eyes penetrating deep into my soul. I moaned in response to his feverish kiss, my body pulsing from the onslaught, my hands taking him in thankful ownership, working their way around his waist, up the sculpted form of his back and shoulders.

His fingers slid into the hair at my nape and pulled tight, cocking my head back roughly to force my gaze. "You're not alone, Ella." He paused, his eyes searching mine. "Don't.

Ever. Fucking. Leave us. We'll find you every time. Do you understand?"

"Yes. Please..."

His mouth crashed back to mine, desperate orders spewed into our kiss... "You'll stay. You'll never leave. You're mine, Ella."

His large body overtook me, forcing me onto the bed. The sight of him crawling over the top of me sent my pulse racing in anticipation. The feel of his weight was intoxicating as he lowered his lips passionately to mine. I relished in the strength of his body, running my hands along his form, needing to feel all of him. My fingers squeezed and clawed at every perfectly defined muscle. My head screamed to push him away, to hate him, but at the same time, I longed for him. I yearned to forget the shitstorm I'd found myself in, or maybe something was really wrong with me since I couldn't help myself around these Vepar.

Our kiss was hectic, intense. We consumed each other, reaching to the deepest recesses of our mouths, the need to brand each other mutual. Heated, our fingers working in a desperate urgency to touch. Our clothes came off in a whirlwind of hands, tugging and ripping each other's shirts off, before moving to discard our pants. I gasped as he slowly, teasingly slid his hands up my legs, tearing my underwear from my body, eliciting my slight scream.

My gaze darted back to his, and I whimpered at the burning heat emanating from his stare as he slid his muscled form over the top of me, resuming his passionate kisses. Kisses that worked their way down my trembling body, pausing at my chest, my belly button, to tantalize every inch of my skin with savoring licks of his devouring lips and tongue.

"Thane," I moaned as he spread my legs with a firm pull,

my whole body clenching in anticipation of his sinful mouth, but desperate for him to fill it at the same time.

"You're so beautiful," he whispered, kissing my thighs, teasing me with his tongue. "It's like you were made for us. Such a delicate, perfect little human," he sighed out. His words only heightened the sensations that I already drowned in. I needed to hear words like this.

My body bowed to his delicious mercy, and I panted as he continued his ministrations. I grabbed his hair, moaning with every touch. I pulled and urged the return of his lips to mine, missing the feel of them against mine. Everything he did felt out of this world, different but just as good as my night with Derrial. I wondered if it could be like this with any experienced men or were the Vepar just particularly good in bed?

Kissing was incredible, but I needed him inside of me. I pulled him closer to me, trying to signal what I wanted without breaking contact with him. Finally he moved to settle between my legs, his heat scorching hot against my sex.

"You're sure about this?" he asked me, sounding almost like he was in pain as he paused above me.

"Isn't it obvious?" I clasped his face and resumed our frenzied kiss. When he finally thrusted inside of me, our simultaneous moans echoed through the tangle of our lips. He felt euphoric, like he was always meant to be a part of me. Like I've been missing him my entire life.

He glided in and out with precision, his gaze never straying from mine. I was mesmerized by the intensity of the moment. I'd been so full of anger when I was with Darrial. Would it have been like this if I had let myself feel something?

"Is this real?" I whispered as an unwelcome tear slid down my face.

He thrust inside me one more time before responding, watching the tear's descent. "This is the realest thing I've ever felt," he finally answered in a gruff voice that almost sounded as if he was choked up. His words consumed me, and he continued to move in and out of me.

The strength of our connection was to die for, every nerve inside of me awakened at his touch. I bowed uncontrollably, moving in helpless abandonment as the pleasure heightened. Seated fully, he stilled, and lifted his head to stare into my eyes. His blue gaze searched mine. I was speechless. Breathless. The pure emotion reflected in his stare had me sucking in air. There was something there between us, something I couldn't put into words, but I realized I wanted to hear it desperately. We stared at one another for what felt like an eternity until he finally closed his eyes, breaking the moment. When he opened them again, the words were gone.

He brushed his fingers along my forehead, pushing the strands of hair away. His lips started to move, and I pulled his lips back to mine before he could speak. Our bodies said what our lips couldn't. I mewled into his kiss as his thrusts grew faster. My hips met his thrusts, measure for measure, needing him so deep inside me I wasn't sure I'd survive otherwise. We were frenetic in our need for each other, desperate, unable to pull away.

He drew his lips from mine, and instead, he took mock bites out of my flesh across my collarbone. His hand slid beneath my back, pulling me closer. I arched my body towards him, my head falling backward as his lips continued to move down my body.

"Fall for me," he whispered, and his words are my undoing. The sexy timber of his voice combined with the steady tempo of his thrusts sent me plummeting over the precipice. Screaming his name, I slid my hands in his hair, gripping hard, riding the overwhelming waves of pleasure, convulsing uncontrollably. His thrusts pounded relentlessly as I rode the ebbs and flows, in and out, deeper and deeper into my clutching depths, before he finally stilled above me. He gave a delicious groan as he peppered my face and neck with kisses.

Harsh breaths amid the grasp of each other's arms, we awaited the slowing of our rapid heartbeats in euphoric silence. Sliding out of me, he chuckled at my elicited whimper, turning to his side on the mattress, pulling me with him.

"I'm not done with you yet, sweetheart," he warned playfully, running his fingers gently along my sweat-slickened back.

"I hope you'll never be," I admitted shyly.

His eyes widened at my admission, and I worried for a second, I'd said too much.

"Good," he replied, giving me a sexy grin. He wrapped me in his arms, lifting me up with ease, moving to stand. "Time for a shower." He smirked, as he carried me to the bathroom, holding me in one strong arm, and leaning in to turn it on.

"Thank you for saving me," I whispered to him as the steam from the hot water began to envelop us, making me feel as if we were in our own little world and the outside world and all of its problems didn't exist.

"Always," he answered.

It was a long, long time before we said anything else.

~

I WAS ALONE when I woke up, the house perfectly still around me. I shuddered at the feeling of being alone, my feelings unreasonably hurt at the fact that Thane had left me after the night we'd shared.

Getting out of bed, I wandered to the window. It was a dreary day, so cloudy that it looked later than it actually was. With my stomach rumbling, I pulled on the only pair of sweats in my closet and wandered downstairs, and through the rooms on my way to the kitchen.

I searched for a sign of Thane or of corran but they weren't around. I finally made it to the kitchen, also deserted. Opening the fridge, the first thing I noticed was the bowl of blueberries. It had only been a few days since I fell in a pile of blueberries, getting choked by Thane. My how things had changed. Maybe something was wrong with me? I'd adjusted so quickly to everything...had even slept with two of them after being terrorized by them for weeks. Thane had literally choked me right outside this kitchen. And here I was, casually eating breakfast instead of trying to get away like any normal girl. Was I so desperate for affection of any kind that I had latched on to the first sign of it? This was literally the species that I believed was responsible for my parent's disappearance.

My appetite had disappeared with my morose thoughts, so I closed the refrigerator and wandered into the other rooms in the house. I decided to explore the house a bit more to get my mind off things. I could wonder if I was sick in the head at some other point. After yesterday I needed a day off.

I walked through the rooms, stopping to admire the expensive artwork on the walls. I'd been in a hurry to find an exit the last time I had explored the house and I hadn't had time to admire the fact that there was a movie theater and workout room that was the size of the gym that I attended near home.

I was strolling through the library filled with more books than I had ever seen in one place, and was about to leave, when I noticed a section of the wall that looked like it stuck out farther than everywhere else.

Walking over I realized that the wall seemed to be sticking out farther because it was some kind of disguised door, and it had been left open. Peeking through the crack I spied a steep staircase leading to an open area. I opened the door a little wider and listened for a moment, trying to see if I could hear any voices coming from down below. I couldn't hear anything. Ignoring the voice in my head that said I should leave it alone; I opened the door wider and started to descend. I paused every couple of steps to see if I could hear anything, and then would continue on when everything remained silent. I had been searching for a reason for their arrival, so maybe I'd finally stumbled across the answer. Excitement tangled in my gut, layered with fear over getting caught.

When I reached the bottom of the steps, I stared around in amazement. Out of everything that I had seen related to the Vepar, this room was the most "out of this world" yet. Sleek, silver tables were set up with hologram images projecting out of them. There was one table that displayed what looked like about 100 different screens showing different parts of the world. Another table had a hologram screen with thousands of numbers scrolling down. I examined the 100 plus images for a moment trying to see if there was anything familiar looking, but I couldn't recognize anything.

Skipping the numbers for now I walked over to the left wall which was made up of an enclosed glass bookcase showcasing various specimens in every chamber. I gasped in amazement at some of the creatures that must have been from their planet. A black, spider with twelve legs instead of eight. It was easily three times the size of a tarantula, and I shivered as I watched it eat a mouse whole. There was some kind of purple creature with four eyes, reminding me of the embodiment of the Furby toy that had been popular when I was a child.

There were also things that were recognizable and left me shivering. In one chamber sat a human heart... Still beating. In another one was an organ that I was pretty sure were female ovaries. And in another one was a human embryo.

Sickness rose through me, so I finally backed away and headed over to the hologram with all the numbers. There were thousands of digits on the screen, but only two columns fully caught my attention. One said Vepar Female and one said Human Female. The numbers were changing rapidly on the human column. What was it counting? Deaths? Or women attending gyms. I almost laughed at how stupid that sounded. What if it was somehow tracking every birth and death? The Vepar column was barely changing with almost no deaths and no births at all.

I tried to think what they would need such information for. Looking through the other columns I found no columns for males.

"What are you doing in here?" barked an angry sounding Corran from behind me.

My heart skipped in my chest, and I twirled around to see him at the base of the stairs, a red tinge to his very handsome cheeks.

"I was just exploring the house and the door was open," I tried to explain, my voice shaking.

"You shouldn't be down here," he snapped. "Did you touch anything?"

"No, I just looked," I answered, my hands trembling at how angry he sounded. Corran had always only sounded interested or mild-mannered. I hardly recognized the seething Vepar in front of me.

"I'm sorry," I started to say, but he was already pointing to the stairs.

"Get out of here," he yelled, and I didn't waste a second more trying to apologize. I flew up the stairs with tears in my eyes.

I ran into Thane at the top of the stairs. "What were you doing down there?" he demanded.

"I've already been yelled at enough; I don't need you to chime in. I'd almost forgotten I was a prisoner in this place, but I won't be forgetting again," I told him, flying by before he could grab my arm. I ran to my bedroom and slammed the door, wishing there was a way to lock the door from the inside.

Ten minutes ticked by as I pouted on the bed, my mind racing with what had been in that room and the look in Corran's eyes when he'd seen me down there. Why didn't they want me to see whatever those things were measuring?

A knock sounded on my door, startling me from my musings since I hadn't heard anyone climbing the stairs. "Can I come in?" asked Corran through the door.

"No," I belligerently said, knowing that I was acting like a two-year-old even as I said it. He opened the door anyway. I didn't expect anything less because from the beginning the Vepar had done whatever they wanted.

"I'm pretty sure I told you not to come in," I said as he stood at the foot of my bed. I was pleased to see he looked a bit scared of me...and slightly ashamed.

"I came to apologize," he said, fiddling with the bottom of his shirt in a decidedly human gesture.

I continued my childish behavior by not saying anything and just staring at him stonily.

"I'm sort of a rarity on Vepar," he continued, when he saw that I wasn't going to say anything. "Our scientists have for the most part been able to eradicate any abnormalities or disorders that used to be present in the Vepar genetic line. My parents were Vepar that were a part of the last nomadic clan though, so they hadn't been subject to any of the genetic cleansing like the rest of the population. I have a disorder most similar to your human Obsessive-Compulsive Disorder. When I saw you down there, all I could think about was that you had touched something, and it was out of the order I kept it in." He took a deep breath and looked at me beseechingly, "I had no intention of scaring you, Ella."

Sorrow flooded his gaze as he stood there, and my anger ebbed. I remembered a classmate in high school who'd suffered from OCD. He couldn't walk out of a room without tapping the side of the door three times and he had to walk three steps behind someone at all times if he was walking in the hallway. He'd been the nicest guy, and I remember how much it bothered him to have all these things to do to stay sane. If Corran's mental issues were anything similar to that, I wasn't surprised he grew so mad when he found me down there.

"I really am sorry for going into the room. My parents always used to tell me I was too curious for my own good." I smiled, feeling a momentary pang at the thought of my parents. For a second, I was tempted to ask if he knew anything about their disappearance, but I pushed the thought away. I hadn't seen any sign that they were in the business of kidnapping older humans...only ones they seemed to be sexually attracted to.

Anyway, I did feel like I had the right to ask what was going on in that room. Everything about the gadgets was strange...including the fact that they might be tracking human and Vepar females.

"So, the hologram that I was looking at down there... It looked like it was recording births and deaths of human females," I asked hesitantly, watching Corran carefully to gauge his reaction.

He sighed and sat down on the bed, turning his face away from me as he gazed out the window. "We came to this planet because our planet is dying and killing off our females in the process. Doesn't help that Khonsu have killed so many of our females as well. We've spent hundreds of years searching space to find a planet that would be similar enough to Vepar for us to relocate. We'd heard about Earth, but we also learned that females were in danger here. Part of my job on the planet was to monitor Earth to ensure the same thing happening to our females is not replicated here."

"How does the planet dying affect your females?" I asked, my eyes widened with everything he was saying.

He sighed. It was a heavy sigh filled with frustration. "We're not quite sure. But since the only connection we have to the Vepar woman dying is our planet also dying, we decided that we needed to find other options."

"Other options like finding new planets to inhabit?" I asked, dread growing inside of me.

He nodded.

I looked at him amazed that he'd so casually told me their plan. Up to now they'd been firm with the message that they were here in peace. But obviously that was all a lie.

He must have seen the growing panic in my face because

his eyes widened, and he threw up his hands as if to calm me down. "We're not planning to takeover. We want to share the planet. All of the rules that have been put in place have been to help sustain the planet and make life better in preparation for the Vepar arrival."

I studied his face. He seemed to be telling the truth but Corran had always seemed to have that air of trustworthiness about him from the beginning. For all I knew, he could have been the best liar out of all of them.

"You had no problem taking me without my permission, and you've pretty much taken over Earth," I said bitterly. "Why should I believe that you wouldn't do something else?"

He pursed his lips in frustration before checking his watch. "I have to leave right now on a short expedition I've had planned for months, and I'd like you to come with me. We can talk more on the trip. I'm sure you'd like to get out of the house too."

Corran and I hadn't had the time together that I had experienced with the others. It still felt awkward between us, and the thought of going somewhere with him made me feel more awkward than anything. But I did want to find out more about the Vepar's plans and he seemed to be much more willing to provide me with information than Derrial or Thane were. So, I might be able to uncover more secrets, maybe even if my parents' disappearance had anything to do with them. I decided to go.

Corran was already pulling me behind him before I had even said yes. Evidently the scientist was just as pushy as the others. Before I knew it, I'd found myself standing next to the helicopter pad that had housed the helicopter I'd flown in with Derrial. The helicopter evidently was being used however as the pad stood empty. I looked at Corran quizzically, wondering what we were waiting for, but he was oblivious to my look. He took out a silver contraption that looked like a car fob and pressed a button.

Suddenly, the pad seemed to dissolve and a sleek silver machine that resembled a cross between a car and a small airplane came up on a pedestal like a scene out of Batman. I gasped in amazement, but Corran, unperturbed as always, gave me no explanation as he began pulling me towards the machine. As we approached the contraption, an entryway appeared in the side of the machine and a set of stairs appeared out of nowhere. I stopped abruptly.

"What is this thing?" I asked, needing answers before I got into the machine.

Corran looked at me confused. "Isn't it obvious? This is how we travel. I guess you could say it's our version of an airplane if you had to label it, but the term really doesn't do it justice since it can travel through any terrain including water."

I stared at him incredulously, then the machine. "Wow."

He began to ascend the steps, and then looked at me with a raised eyebrow when I didn't follow him. I was still in shock about the fact that I was about to travel in an alien spacecraft.

"We're on a schedule," he said impatiently, jarring me from my thoughts. I tentatively followed him up the steps, stopping on each one to make sure that they didn't disappear. Once inside I couldn't help but freeze again.

Everything was black as if I'd crawled inside a licorice jelly bean. The walls, ceiling, seats, and even the controls. Light drenched the inside of the shuttle, and the sleek walls glimmered under the right illumination. No other windows lined the rectangular ship.

Corran took the single seat in the front with the controls,

and I slid into one of two available in the back. Buckling up, I couldn't believe where I was, and what I'd give right now to have my phone to snap photos. I was pretty sure if I shared them, my social followers would leap from a measly thirty to millions.

Anyone who shared images revealing anything about the Vepar went viral because they were so secretive. If only people knew something more dangerous lingered amid them. The Khonsu. Then again, maybe that would just cause unnecessary panic because everyone would be safe unless they were compatible like me. Lucky me.

My thoughts turned to the bomb Corran had dropped on me about their race looking for a new home. That information was massive and could easily end up with us going to war with them because the rest of the planet coming here would be construed as a complete take over. I didn't know what to do with such knowledge as it was still processing in my head on what it meant. I mean I knew what it meant, but the situation seemed delicate and I could sympathize with them wanting to save their race. Plus, I didn't want to cause a universal war when I didn't understand all the facts myself, especially when I was pretty sure that humans didn't have a chance against the Vepar technology.

I sucked in a deep breath to calm myself.

"You ready?" Corran glanced over his shoulder at me, his eyes alive, clear he was in his element right here.

"Let's do this before I change my mind." I laughed, but it wasn't a lie either.

A light vibration buzzed under my feet, followed by a brittle silence, but we lifted into the air with such ease and swiftness that I barely felt it. When we finally took off, the vessel moved as if there was no sound, no wind, and it didn't even disturb the air. We glided seamlessly through the air, and my earlier worries faded, replaced by a tingling excitement. My knees bounced and I gawked outside, wanting to stand near Corran to see everything, but I didn't dare move.

Unlike Derrial, who'd talked my ear off during the whole flight on the helicopter, Corran didn't say a word. Instead, he spent the entire time on a tablet that would have looked like an iPad if it weren't for the fact that it projected holographic, 3D images much like the tables in that secret room. Numbers and charts all detecting what looked like other aircrafts.

We traveled for twenty minutes before the machine started to drop smoothly out of the sky. My stomach lurched to my throat, and I clutched my seat belt, surprised how fast we'd arrived, but then again, I suspected we traveled quicker than planes.

When we landed, all I could see out the front window was darkness and the bright starry sky as far as the eye could see. Where in the world were we?

The front door opened with a rush of hot air, hissing in the process. And before us stood a mountain covered with tropical looking trees. This didn't look like anywhere near home.

I hopped out and Corran followed behind me.

"Where are we?"

He took my hand and drew me closer to the mountain. "We're at the edge of a crater."

"Wait!" I pulled against his hand. "Like in a volcano?" It did feel hotter here, the heat so intense it was singeing my skin.

He smiled and moved closer, cupping my face. With a kiss that shocked me, he whispered, "Would you have preferred if I took you to a beach?"

I shrugged and nodded. "Actually yes."

"Well, we might have time after this. We are in Honolulu."

My feet froze, eyes growing. "Are you kidding me? I've always wanted to go to Hawaii. I could have brought my swimsuit."

He broke into a laugh, the sound so soft and sweet that I ate it up. I adored the way he laughed. "Then we better hurry up and get this job done."

14

*T*he grainy sand was almost white, speckled with tiny rocks along the shore. It may be close to midnight in Honolulu, but the moon hung low and was heavy with silver light, beaming off the silent sea like a jewel. Corran had finished collecting samples from the volcano crater, and true to his word, he took me swimming.

"You look spectacular," he said, and I glanced over at him, still in his jeans and buttoned up shirt looking proper as always. At least he'd removed his shoes.

I looked down at myself in a swimsuit we'd found at one of a handful of stores still open. A skinny black bikini, barely covering the sides of my breasts and so skimpy that I might as well have been naked in the back. Corran had surprised me by insisting I wear it. I tried to tell myself that I didn't adore the way his eyes glinted when he stared at me, eating me up with his gaze.

"Why do you enjoy dunking yourself in cold, salty water?" he asked.

"Stop analyzing everything." I grabbed his hand and drew him toward the water lapping across the shore. "It's such a hot night, and it's refreshing to go swimming, especially with someone else." I winked his way. "Especially when the two of us combined should be wearing a lot less clothes than you are right now." I eyed him head to toe.

"If you're implying sex, the friction is painful in water."

I sighed and hauled him closer to the water. "Just follow my direction, okay?"

And to my surprise he nodded.

The water rushed toward us, running up and over my feet. I giggled and latched onto Corran's arm, while he stood there, the hems of his jeans getting wet. He didn't seem to notice as he kept staring at me.

"What?"

"Something in your face looks different when you smile today." He watched me closely, or more like studied me. Corran was always trying to work me out, while me... I just wanted to laugh for a change, stop being afraid.

"It's called freedom." And the moment the words fell from my mouth, an awkwardness fell over me because he was my captor and I wasn't really free. After our time together with him carefully explaining all the data he was collecting on the volcano, I'd foolishly let myself imagine that our situation had changed. All because he'd made me feel incredible in his company, trusting me to help him, taking me to the beach, spoiling me. The hard facts remained however that I remained under his control.

I turned away from him and faced the ocean, my hand slipping out of his grasp. Out in front of me, the dark waters came in gentle waves, proving that nothing would ever tame the ocean.

Corran placed a hand on my shoulder, his touch sizzling hot. "Did I do something wrong?"

When I met his gaze over my shoulder, his lips curled

upward, and he reached over cupping the side of my face so tenderly I almost let myself believe he truly cared.

"On my home planet, women are worshipped and adored. We protect them above all else, and we keep them close at all times to ensure they are safe. But you say freedom like claiming you is wrong."

"Are you listening to what you're saying?" I said, my mouth hanging open from his response.

"Earth is no longer the place you once experienced," he retorted. "And it will never be the same. We've offered you freedom from what is coming," he growled, his expression darkening, and in a heartbeat his features schooled, and his words faded as if he'd said too much. "Go, have your swim, we have to leave soon," he snapped.

I turned and headed into the waters feeling less than a person because the Vepar had this way of giving, then taking away any good they did. Always reminding me of my place. If they revered females so much, why dominate them? My stomach churned with his last words about Earth never being the same again. Something was happening, and it had to do with the test results I found in their secret lab, I felt it in my bones. Regardless of what Corran told me, I wasn't sure how much I could believe. After all, they'd arrived here, shrouded in secrets, so why would he so easily divulge their information? Nope... more secrets lay hidden, and I had every intention to find them out. If I was stuck with them, hidden from another monster, then I'd at least uncover the truth.

The cool water lapped around my thighs and I pushed deeper into the water, dunking myself into the sea's embrace, the iciness refreshing. There was an eeriness about floating in water so dark I couldn't see my hand just below the surface. Who knew what swam around me...

but was that any different to being in the company of Vepar?

I stared back to Corran. He leaned against a palm tree, arms folded over his broad chest, watching me. What would he do if I dove under and never resurfaced? Probably drain the ocean to find me. I would laugh if I didn't believe he'd do exactly that.

I left the water behind, my skin pricked with the cold. Corran hadn't moved from his position even though the towel he'd purchased lay right by his feet. Instead, he drank me in from my head to toes, his sights fastened on my breasts in the skimpy bikini, at my pebbled nipples. When I reached his side, he picked up the towel and dusted it of sand before wrapping it around my shoulders. He rubbed the fabric over my arms and back to dry me. His moves were smooth and unaffected, but his eyes held a hunger that showed how he truly was feeling.

He leaned down and kissed me, his lips on fire. His breathing escalated and he held onto my shoulder while another hand cupped my breast. With deft fingers, he peeled back the material, revealing one of my breasts. Then he bent over further, collecting it into his mouth.

I gasped, glancing around to see if anyone was around. Finding we were alone I relaxed although the knowledge that we could get caught still filled me with a nervous thrill. His hands fell to my backside and he kneaded my cheeks. The way he sucked on my chest had me swooning, arousal escalating quickly through me, my head fogged with heat. And he wasn't letting me go either, plucking at my flesh with his lips.

"Corran," I breathed, fire scorching hot between my thighs. As if sensing my need, his fingers found the edge of my bikini bottoms and slid inside. Caressing me softly, he slowly slid into me. I parted my legs slightly for easier access, only the towel sitting on my back like a cape concealing what was going on if anyone watched. My cheeks sizzled, but nothing compared to the heat I felt that he was touching me so intimately in public.

I groaned, grasping his shoulders, needing him with every fiber of my being. I ought to be pissed at his treatment of me earlier, but as always, his attentiveness won me over, taking all my anger away.

When he turned me around, driving my back to the palm tree, he ripped the bikini top the rest of the way off. I could barely breathe from need. His mouth latched onto my other breast, eliciting another gasp out of me. His fingers pushed back into my bikini bottoms, and his knee nudged my legs wider.

"We shouldn't do this here," I moaned, staring around us, but when his fingers slipped inside of me again, I lost myself. Gone were all my thoughts, the only thing remaining was a desperate desire to float on the clouds. His tongue flicked me and holding out seemed an impossibility. His teeth bit down softly on my flesh, and it all become too much, too fast. I fell over the edge, and a cry of pleasure fell from my mouth, my body shuddering.

Diving into my mouth in a deep kiss, Corran's tongue slayed me, erasing every thought of the outside world until I was breathless, and we had to break away to drag in air. I writhed, soaking, every last inch of desire throttling through me. It took me a few minutes to settle down. Corran kissed me softly before moving away and pulling the towel tightly around my chest. Embracing me once again, I melted into him.

"Come, you must be starved." We began to walk along

the sandy beach of Honolulu. As I stared up at the stars, I knew I would never forget my brief time in Hawaii.

CORRAN HADN'T TOUCHED his Wagyu ribeye, only the vegetables, but even those he only picked at. He seemed miles away as we sat in a restaurant fit for royalty. Embroidered curtains, dark oak tables, sandstone tile floor, and meals were served from silver trays. The restaurant was full, each table bustling, voices buzzing, and a delicate piano played throughout the dimly lit room. I was worried if Corran regretted what had just happened when he finally looked over at me with a smile, the worry he had carried moments earlier vanished.

"You look beautiful." His attention fell to my low v-neck dress, the one he'd bought me once we arrived in New York for a meal. The trip itself was another testament to Vepar technology since Hawaii to New York had only taken thirty minutes. I blushed all over, the earlier fire from the beach surging through me once again, and I grew hot and bothered as I clenched my thighs. It didn't take long for him to affect me, for any of them to affect me, just a simple look did the trick. Something had to be wrong with me to react to the Vepar so fast.

I looked down at the blue gown I wore, it was the color of the night sky with tiny sparkles all over it when the light caught it in the right direction.

I blushed when I looked up and he was still watching me with admiration.

"I'm sure this dress could make even you look handsome," I told him, laughing at myself trying to downplay the fact that he and his friends were the most gorgeous males I had ever seen. Looking around at my surroundings, this place was the most posh and uppity place I had been to in my life. I'd never be able to afford to visit such a place, and if I stepped foot in here without Corran, I'd be marched out. I suspected that the way we had been treated while we were here, like we were royalty, had everything to do with being on the arm of a Vepar.

"I didn't mean to upset you back by the ocean. I've got a few things on my mind," he explained and reached over to take my hand in his. His thumb stroked the back of my wrist in slow, gentle circles. His hair, the color of mahogany, framed his strong face and his eyes reminding me of milky caramel. Despite being the quieter of the three Vepar, the one who analyzed things first and who seemed to calculate everything before he acted, Corran was incredibly handsome in his own way. But unlike the others, he didn't seem to know it.

Despite all the logic in my mind and everything that had happened, I couldn't help but fall under his spell each time we exchanged glances. What would it be like to really date someone who looked this perfect...Someone normal. Not an alien with so many secrets it gave him a Dr Jekyll and Mr. Hyde personality. I wanted to look past that, to believe Corran meant well.

"Feel like talking about it?"

He sighed heavily. "Some things are better left unsaid."

I wasn't sure if that was one of his riddles I had to decipher, or he was speaking directly this time.

He flinched and reached for his pocket, before pulling out a ringing cell. "Give me a moment." He was on his feet and marching outside with the phone pressed to his ear before I could respond.

Glancing down at my half-eaten gnocchi, I pierced one

with my fork and ate it, loving the buttery taste. Why hadn't I tried these before?

Eating could only distract me for so long and I couldn't prevent my thoughts from thinking about the complicated situation I had found myself in. For so long my life has been about living to get through the day and into the next. With these three Vepar, my life had become so much more in such a short time. The deep-seated emotion they awakened in me was enticing, and it makes me want to feel even more. The opportunity to taste any level of the type of intensity they brought into my life was becoming a necessity.

When someone flopped into Corran's seat, I sat up, expecting him, ready to say that was fast, but it wasn't his face I met.

Across from me sat the Devil, and I shuddered in my shoes.

He wore a black jacket, hair oily and slicked off his face, and he had regained that haunting gauntness in his cheeks of the monster who'd tortured me with whips.

I pushed back in an instant, my seat's feet scraping the ground in a terrifying screech, drawing attention from those at nearby tables. My heart pounded in my chest, and I shook, unable to stop remembering the way this bastard had hurt me, took my blood, and threatened to come for me. And here he was, trying it in public.

Shit!

"Don't go," the Khonsu whispered, glancing toward the door where Corran had left moments earlier. I mentally counted the space between me and the exit. Fifteen, maybe sixteen steps.

I jolted to my feet, but he grasped my wrist before I could get anywhere, also standing, his grip as cold and solid as iron.

"Sit!" he growled beneath his breath, hauling me back to my seat with such force, I stumbled into it, almost sliding off.

Fear pressed down on my chest, squeezing my lungs as he held onto my wrist, not letting go.

I was never going to be left alone. I would always be hunted. I hated this. I loathed the constant terror.

"What do you want?" I snapped, wrestling to free my hand, but he didn't budge.

"Tonight, you're not my prey," he murmured, his gaze flipping back and forth from the door to me, and I prayed Corran returned fast.

"What do you mean?" I asked.

"I have some information I think you would be interested in," he replied, picking up Corran's dinner knife and casually inspecting it as if it held interesting information.

"I can't think of anything you could tell me that would interest me except why you're stalking me." My words came out brave, but inside I was trembling. I set my napkin purposely on my knife and slipped both off the table. I gripped the knife hard under the table determined that when he did try to take me, I would fight back.

"Little human, what have they told you about why the Vepar are on Earth?" he asked.

I studied him wondering why it mattered. "The Vepar are here because their planet is dying and it's making their females sick."

"Ever wondered why they seem to care so much about the health of human females?" he said with a sly grin. His question dug in deep to the issues that I had tried to push from my mind.

I said nothing and his grin widened. "The Vepar women are barren," he stated in a matter of fact tone. "And even though the Vepar have long lives, so long that some would consider them immortal, their numbers are still dwindling without any hope of replacement." My eyes widened. It had been something that I suspected ever since seeing the graphs in their basement room, but the way Corran had talked to me so earnestly had made me want to not question him. Corran seemed the most trustworthy of the three of them, but what if he was the best liar of them all?

I shook my head. Why was I even deigning to listen to anything that this creature was saying? A creature who had cruelly tortured me for no reason other than I existed.

"Trying to convince yourself that I'm lying?" he asked with a chuckle. "Your three males are three of the most powerful Vepar in their society. To get in that position, don't you think there has to be something a little bit more special to make them stand out in a race that prides itself on superiority?"

My trembling grew. I didn't know what was coming next, but I knew I was going to hate it.

"They're going to breed you," he whispered to me. "Corran discovered how to make a Vepar embryo be accepted into a human female. Thanks to you."

"Thanks to me?" I said, my voice sounding horrified even to me. "Your blood had the magic touch," he said with a shrug. "There's a whole list of you with the same special chromosome that will allow for you to birth little Vepar."

"You mean hybrids, right? Half human, half Vepar?" I asked, thinking that it wouldn't be so bad if the three of them loved me and we wanted to have children someday.

He laughed. It was a dark laugh filled with glee over my ignorance. "No, little human. They plan on knocking you out and putting in embryos just like you humans do with surrogates. Then they're going to keep you hooked on machines like true breeders until the birth of the Vepars. And then, when you've done your job and continued their race, you're going to die."

I stared at him, dread threatening to choke me. My mind was having trouble trying to fathom how what he was saying could even be real. An image came to my mind of me strapped with a pregnant belly on a gurney in a tank with tubes coming out of me. I wanted to throw up.

A shadow fell over our table, and I jumped in my seat, so on edge, I was ready to scream.

Corran towered over us, and relief crashed through me. But before I could take another breath, he grabbed the Khonsu by the throat and hurled him across the room. Our table lifted from the alien's feet kicking in resistance and flew sideways.

And then, panic broke out.

Screams. People running toward the exit, fear gripping their expressions. Chairs and food flying across the room from where the two aliens fought. And this wasn't just punches and fists, but a battle between two animals. They charged for one another, headbutting, throwing one another against the walls.

Each time Corran fell, I curled over, hugged myself, the idea of him in pain feeling like a blade to my heart.

Every inch of me trembled, and I sat in my chair, frozen with the chaos erupting in the restaurant.

Get out, my mind yelled. I finally leaped to my feet, my muscles high on pure adrenaline. I felt nothing but the urgency to escape drumming through my veins. The grip of panic pushed me, my brain synapses fired away scenario after scenario on how I could die here tonight, but it also came with the idea that this might be my chance to escape.

I felt horrible leaving Corran this way, drowning in a

scuffle of grunts and snarls, of blood and aggression, but what could I do? I didn't even have a phone to call the other two Vepar for backup.

So, I ran. It was something I was good at.

I pushed past the overturned tables and chairs, pushing myself into the bottleneck of people squeezing out the door. Cries of terror surrounded me, and my heart beat faster and harder listening to everyone panic.

I burst out onto the sidewalk with the horde, and I swung right, away from the direction of the shuttle. While I had no idea where I was going, I just knew I had to run. I shoved past people, my mind racing with the need to find a place to hide.

"Ella?" A female's voice cried out, but I didn't look back, I didn't dare.

When someone grabbed my arm, I flinched around, hands fisted, ready to fight. But when I saw Cherry standing there, holding onto me, wearing a strapless dress, her hair curled, and dark makeup around her cerulean eyes, I let out a light cry.

My mouth gaped open at bumping into her.

"Shit, girl, where the hell have you been, and what are you wearing?"

My throat thickened, and despite our past, I leaped into her arms, not caring about anything as it felt incredible to see a familiar face, to feel some connection to the life I thought I'd lost.

She pushed me off her. "What's going on? I've called you for days, and when I went to visit you, the landlord said he'd kicked you out and was selling your stuff to pay for your unpaid rent." Gripping her hips, she glared at me, waiting for an explanation.

My heart sunk through me, but I didn't have time for

this. "Listen, can we go to your place now? I have so much to tell you, but I'm in danger."

Her brow pinched. "I'm here with friends. But you can make it up to me tomorrow by taking me out to brunch."

I shook my head and glanced up the sidewalk behind her where the mass of people hovered near the restaurant. "Please, Cherry. For me, do this for me. I never ask you for anything."

She rolled her eyes. It seemed she hadn't changed much. In that moment I finally realized how stupid I had been to ever consider her my real friend.

"Forget it," I snapped and whipped around to run.

Instead, I crashed into a wall of stone muscle. And when I looked up into Corren's bloody and furious face, I winced.

Oh, fuck.

"Who's this guy?" Cherry purred behind me, and was she really flirting?

But I couldn't move. My feet were glued to the sidewalk with dread.

"I told you you're ours!" And he leaned over, snatching me up before tossing me over his shoulder as if I were a sack.

I screamed and slapped my hands across his back, but people just stared at us, doing nothing.

Corran's large hands held down my legs, one hand on my ass, and he hiked it back toward the ship.

Cherry stared at me in shock.

"I've been kidnapped, help!" I yelled at her. But she simply stared after me, a shocked and jealous look on her face. The last thing I saw before we turned the corner was her making a call on her phone.

What the fuck!

15

——————

$\mathcal{I}$ slouched in my room in the dark, staring out the window at the night sky. I was back at the manor again. Corran hadn't said a word after he'd dragged me kicking and screaming to the roof of a nearby building where his plane was waiting for us. I didn't bother explaining why I'd ran or try to make any excuses. The Khonsu's words had spread through my mind like poison, and once again I found myself thinking of the Vepar as the enemy rather than the lovers I had begun to think of them as.

We landed and Corran had grabbed my arm roughly before practically dragging me into the house and up the stairs to my room. He threw me onto the bed and turned to leave the room.

"So, I'm a prisoner again?" I asked, my feelings irrationally hurt at his treatment of me even though I never should have expected anything else.

"You ran, again. That doesn't earn you any privileges."

"So everything that's happened wasn't real?" I asked, my

voice clogged with the tears that I was desperately trying to keep at bay.

His eyes closed for a second as if my question pained him, but when they opened again, they were as cold as ever.

"Just stay put," he said exasperatedly, storming out and slamming the door behind him. Surprisingly, I didn't hear the lock engage. After his footsteps faded, signaling he'd gone down the stairs, I walked to the door to check it. Sure enough, it wasn't locked.

Feeling slightly mollified, I went back to my bed and laid down, the intensity of the day suddenly catching up to me and making me realize how exhausted I felt. Every inch of me ached.

And that's what I had been doing for the last few hours.

As I laid on the bed, my mind continued to obsess over what the Khonsu had said. I had to know for myself if it was true. Asking the Vepar obviously wasn't going to work since they had already told me the story, they wanted me to believe. No, if I was going to find out, I was going to have to do it myself. And I was pretty sure that the answers to my questions lay in that secret room.

I waited until the middle of the night. I still wasn't sure about Vepar sleeping habits, but I knew that they at least slept for a few hours based on my experience with Derrial in the D.C. hotel room.

Once the clock struck two a.m., I carefully tiptoed to the door and slowly opened it, pausing every couple of inches to listen. When the house remained quiet, I opened the door all the way and slipped out into the hallway. My heartbeat felt unnaturally loud as I crept through the hallways. The journey seemed to take forever since my entire body was on hyper alert sure that one of the Vepar was going to appear at any moment.

I finally made it into the library, and I fumbled with the bookshelf where the hidden door was located for a few minutes, trying to figure out how to open it since it had already been opened last time. My hand finally slipped across a book towards the bottom of the bookshelf that when pulled, released the door. The door creaked as it slid open and my heart stopped as I listened, nervously expecting to hear the sound of feet coming down the hallway.

Five minutes passed and then ten and I finally got the nerve to continue. I slipped down the stairs, the lights automatically coming on as I entered the room.

Everything looked as it did the other day. The holograms still glowed from where they were suspended in the air above the tables. There were still creepy creatures on the side wall. Yes, everything looked the same, but I was sure that somewhere in here was the answer to my questions.

I ran my hand over all the surfaces thinking that there had to be some hidden button that would show me something. When that didn't work, I searched every nook and cranny in the room to try and find another hidden passageway.

After thirty minutes of searching, I wandered over to the table with the birth and death graphs, frustrated at the fact that I hadn't been able to find anything and would have to leave soon so that they didn't find me. I waved my hand in frustration at the hologram...and to my surprise, the screen changed.

No longer was I staring at changing graphs. Instead I studied what looked to be a medical file.

My medical file in fact, and my stomach dropped. It listed everything about me on the screen. Where I'd gone to school, who was my first kiss, my blood type. I waved the screen again and to my horror a mockup appeared of a chamber that looked similar to the images that had filled my head when the Khonsu had been talking.

The chamber rotated in the air, all the specifications listed in a paragraph below. It was labeled as an "incubator." But I knew that it wasn't going to be hatching eggs...it was going to be growing Vepar.

My stomach ached with each passing second.

I kept scrolling through the various screens. There was more information about my chromosomes. Pictures of Vepar embryos. And on the last screen was a list of names labeled, "Probable Subjects." I was the very last name on the list.

It was one thing to hear about such a scenario, but to actually see evidence of a plan to make human women into Vepar surrogates was almost more than I could comprehend. And here I let myself have feelings for these aliens, and I was nothing more than a lab experiment.

Stumbling backwards away from the hologram screen, barely able to take breath into my lungs, I spun to get out of the room.

Much to my horror, Thane was standing in the doorway, a menacing look capturing his expression. Narrowing eyes and a pinched nose, he grunted. And with his curled shoulders, he was beyond pissed.

Dread squeezed around my chest, and I could barely take a breath.

"Find something interesting, pet?" he growled.

I looked widely around the room, my mind desperately trying to come up with scenarios of how I could escape...what excuse I could use.

Thane was upon me in a flash, and I screamed. The last

thing I saw was him raising a small black device up to my neck as I struggled to get away.

Then, everything went black.

To Be Continued in Broken. Get your copy at books2read.com/fallenworld2

Authors' Note

C.R. Jane

It was such a great experience working with Mila on my first co-write ever. It's come at the best time since sharing the writing load helps a lot during my pregnancy right now. I'm so grateful for all our readers. This was a departure from what I normally write but as we came up with the story, I knew it was going to be fantastic. I love sci-fi. I grew up on Star Trek and even though this one is set on earth; I loved the idea of working with aliens. We have an amazing series planned, and I can't wait to show you what's in our crazy brains!

Mila Young

Thank you to all the incredible and inspirational readers who've joined me on my writing journey from the beginning and for spending time with my imagination. Bound was an incredibly fun and rewarding tale to write with C.R. Jane, our creativities blending to bring you a sci-fi romantic tale about what could happen should Earth ever be visited by another race of beings. You will love what we have planned for this series, so join us on this voyage to experience the unimaginable, the beautiful, and how love can be found in the most unlikeliest of places.

Keep reading for a look at Lamented Pasts, Book 1 of the Timeless Affection Series

Lamented Pasts

Loneliness. That's all Juliet Caris has ever known. Cursed to pass through time, Juliet is at the whims of fate.

Changing centuries without warning, she's fallen in love...

With a blacksmith...

And a future king.

With a soldier...

And with a mobster.

Each time, she finds herself yanked out of time...and away from her love.

A piece of her heart has been lost to the men she has left behind at every stop she has made, and finding herself once again alone, she believes she has no parts of herself left to give. Now she seeks out the graves of the men she used to love, trying to convince herself that she won't glimpse them again in the street.

Their love felt timeless...but surely, only she is.

Can a new man with the same powerful pull on her heart she's found so many times before bring her back to life and help her regain what she has lost through the centuries?

Or will Juliet disappear from his life...and this time, disappear for good?

PROLOGUE

Boston, U.S.A. 2018

The stone is worn and almost impossible to read, a reminder of the hundreds of years that separate me from its inhabitant. I've searched for it for a year in this lifetime. Just like the others, I had to see the proof that he was gone. I had to make sure that somehow a miracle hadn't happened, and I would stumble upon him somehow in this life. I had to make sure that I wouldn't turn and see him flashing me that heart-stopping grin as he pushed his wayward, russet-colored hair out of his face. He was always laughing about something, usually about some crazy idea I had told him about.

Sometimes, I've imagined that I've seen him. I've found myself running after strangers whose walk, or gestures, or profile reminds me of his. I'll tap the strangers on their shoulders. They turn around expectantly, flashing a smile when they see a pretty face. Their expressions inevitably turn to ones of concern as they uncomfortably ask if I'm alright since I've burst into tears at the sight of their face. It happens every time though. I just haven't been able to stop myself from looking for him.

It won't be a problem after today though. Just like it's not a problem with any of the others.

I trace the dates with the tips of my fingers. 1778. Just five years after I left. I wonder if he died in the war, if another woman watered the ground beneath me with her tears, mourning a life that would never be. That's what I would have done. That's what the tears streaming down my face are for. I'm mourning the death of my last chance for happiness.

Curious tourists pass by me hesitantly. I'm sure wondering how a centuries old gravestone could cause me to weep uncontrollably. Rotting cemeteries aren't supposed to inspire fresh pain. They would never guess that this loss feels just like yesterday to me. I wipe my eyes on my shirt, and press a kiss on my fingers that I then press on the stone.

"Goodbye Gabriel," I whisper softly to the grave, knowing that there will be no closure for me even with the confirmation that he truly is gone.

I walk out of the cemetery, passing laughing families holding American flags, all enjoying a lovely, autumn Saturday. I walk and walk some more, the beauty of Boston invisible to me as I mourn so many lost lifetimes.

I finally stop when I get to the ocean. I close my eyes and soak in the feel of the breeze against my face. It reminds me of all of them, of everything that I have found, and everything that I have lost. The breeze stirs the strands of my hair, brushing them against my skin, almost like a lover's caress.

"No more," I whisper to the sea. It doesn't answer me back.

CHAPTER 1

"Orders up," calls out Val, shaking me out of my reverie.

I give a deep sigh and walk over to the counter to grab the food for my waiting customers. The air is thick with the stench of fried food and sweat. My shoes squeak on the black and white checkered floor as I make my way to one of my tables to deliver their food. Pretending to ignore the table full of truckers' wandering, leering eyes, I set their food down and force a smile at them, politely asking if they need anything else.

"Just your number, baby," says one of them. I involuntarily shiver, the man's got to be pushing sixty and he's missing a few teeth.

"Afraid I can't help you with that, sir," I tell him with a grimace. "Let me know if you need anything related to your meals though." I can feel their continued interest as I walk away, and I know that I'm going to be carrying my bear spray with me when I walk home tonight after my shift is over. You never can be too careful about creepers these days.

My mind automatically thinks of Landon, and how he would insist on picking me up every night if he was here. He would probably have me carrying a gun with me every-where as well. I immediately feel a pang of loss, and I force myself to concentrate on folding napkins while I wait for the rest of my tables to finish.

"We've got a live one," says my co-worker Bethany.

I grunt uninterested, brushing my too-long black hair out of my face.

"You can have it," I tell her. "It's been a slow day."

"Ooh honey, consider this your birthday present for the next five years," she tells me with a wink.

She looks behind me again.

"Make that the next ten years," she says, giving me a little push in the direction of where the newcomer assumedly just sat down.

I sigh, but can't help but give her a returning grin. Bethany is the quintessential cougar. Mid-fifties, with the tendency to wear her eye makeup a little too dark, and her hair a little too big, she keeps me laughing on the daily. She's the only bright spot in this shitty diner I've found myself working at. It's a little hard to get a good job when you're never around a place long enough to get a degree. Not that a degree from the last place I was at would get me anywhere here. Well, maybe an insane asylum.

I can see the concerned look on the doctors' faces in my head right now.

"So, you're actually saying that you believe you've just returned from the 1700s." I have to stop myself from erupting in laughter at that thought. I sober up when I see Bethany's concerned look.

"Oh sweetie, when are you going to start living in the present?" she asks me sadly.

I can't help but tear up at her concerned tone. 'Never' is the answer, but I can't tell her that.

"I'm fine, just tired. You know I've been working a lot of shifts lately," I tell her reassuringly. I know she sees right through me, but she smiles at me anyway.

"Go make that fine piece of ass's dreams come true," she says, flouncing away in her cheap, leopard heels that are at least five inches tall. It's a wonder that she can stand on her feet all day with as much as we walk around in this job.

I'm still laughing as I turn and start walking to the new customers. My laugh dies in my throat when I lock eyes with one of the table's occupants.

Green. That's what first strikes me. His eyes are so green that they almost glow in his face. I've never seen someone with eyes that color before. It reminds me of the green of England, a color so vibrant that I can still see it in my mind even though it's been almost forever since I've been back. The rest of him is just as striking. Sandy blonde hair that's haphazardly swept off his face like some girl just finished grabbing it in a moment of passion. Lips perfectly full and lush, and currently curled up in a smirk as we continue to stare each other down. He's beautiful.

And I'm not waiting on his table.

I turn quickly around to see where Bethany went, but she's already helping another table. I look around the room, trying to see if anyone else can help me out, knowing that it's an exercise in futility. Bethany and I are the only ones on duty tonight, so unless I want to go drag the crotchety owner of the place out of the back office, I'm going to have to suck it up.

I take a deep breath, put on a fake but polite grin, and walk towards the table.

I've been so caught up with Mr. Perfect at the table that I completely miss the fact that the rest of his table is full of other guys. All are good looking in their own way, but none of them hold a candle to the man who is currently still staring at me intensely. I notice that they are all dressed well, something that you don't see hardly ever in a place like this. We cater more to the down on their luck, rather than the lucky of the population. And this table of men could most definitely be classified as lucky.

"Welcome to Charlie's. What can I get you all to drink today?" I ask them, keeping my eye contact averted from the veritable force of nature I can feel to the right of me.

The men had been laughing at something before I got to the table, but they're all quiet and staring at me acutely now. It doesn't give me pause. I know I'm a beautiful girl. Being loved so completely over the course of my many lifetimes has driven that fact into me. It would be a slap in all of my loves' faces to doubt that fact now.

Unlike the decaying bones of my lovers, I never age. Perfectly preserved it seems for time and all eternity, the youthful glow of my early twenties is all I will ever know.

My attention flits back to the table as each man orders a drink. My stomach gives an involuntary clench when the green-eyed god at the table opens his mouth to give his order.

"Water, no ice," he says, in a voice like chocolate, so rich and deep my cheeks flush.

One of the guys at the table chuckles and I curse my pale skin as I skitter away to collect their drink orders.

The next hour passes in agony. The men are polite, talking quietly amongst themselves as I bring them their food and refill their drinks. They aren't inappropriate with me, but I feel *his* gaze on me no matter where I am in the room. It feels suffocating.

It isn't until after they have paid their bill and left that I can finally breathe again. But I'm also filled with a sense of loss.

The rest of my shift passes with little excitement. I wave goodbye to Bethany as I walk out of the diner. She's still rolling silverware and I'm tempted to stay and help, but I've done my fair share for the day and my feet hurt. I can't afford a car, and I need every bit of my tips for my bills for the month, so a cab is out of the question. Thus, I've still got about a two mile walk ahead of me. I square my shoulders and set out into the brisk, autumn night.

I'm just about to cross the street in front of the diner when a long, sleek, black limo pulls out from somewhere and begins to drive towards me. It's sorely out of place on this side of town, and I wonder what it's doing here. Annoyed when it stops right in front of me, I move to walk around it. Suddenly, one of the windows rolls down. Even in the dark, his bright green eyes stand out.

"Need a ride?" he asks.

A ride would actually be wonderful but I'm definitely not getting into a limo, late at night, with someone who seems to be stalking me since he and his buddies left hours ago.

"No thanks," I say, hurrying to go around the limo. The door opens up and he gets out, blocking my way.

"What can I say to convince you?" he asks, flashing a charming smile.

"Nothing," I reply. "I'm not in the habit of taking rides from strangers."

He holds out a hand.

"My name is Liam," he says. "Now as soon as you tell me

your name we won't be strangers and I can give you a ride home."

"How long have you been waiting out here?" I ask, ignoring his request for my name.

"Your friend in there was only too happy to let me know what time you got off of your shift," he tells me with a smirk.

I'm going to kill Bethany tomorrow. If this delicious looking stalker doesn't kill me first.

"I'm sorry, but I have to go," I tell him, maneuvering to go around him. Just then there's a bolt of lightning that flashes across the sky. It's immediately followed by the crash of thunder. I look up just as the clouds decide to release the torrent of water they've been threatening us with all day.

"Just let me give you a ride," he yells over the pounding rain, holding out his hand.

We're both getting soaked, and even though I know I shouldn't, the thought of walking miles in this storm, in the only uniform I have, finally leads to me nodding in agreement.

He seems to sigh in relief, before pulling me unexpectedly towards the limo. I crawl into its plush interior, flinching at the leather seats that are going to be destroyed by the water dripping off my body. He follows close behind me and then shuts the door. We sit there staring at one another in silence.

He pushes his soaking, wet hair out of his eyes, and smiles tentatively.

"Will you give me your name now?" he asks.

"Juliet," I tell him stiffly.

"That wasn't so hard now, was it?"

I don't respond. He's dangerous, and not just because he's a stranger. His combination of charm and wickedly good looks is not something I want to deal with right now.

I pause before answering, deciding that I'll have him drop me off at the Walmart down the street from my dilapidated apartment, so he won't know where I live. I may have gotten into a limo with the hottie stranger, but I'm not going to be entirely stupid.

I rattle off the address and he seems to give me a knowing look before pressing a button and telling the driver, assumedly through a speaker, where we are going.

"Why did you come to the diner?" I finally ask, after a long silence where the only sound is the rain hitting the roof of the limo.

"I grew up around here," he says, gesturing to the run-down neighborhood full of dilapidated houses we are passing through.

I look at the clearly expensively tailored suit he is wearing and gesture at him quizzically.

He laughs, a deep rumbling laugh that makes me warm inside despite my best intentions.

"It's true. Those were my buddies from high school I was eating with. We meet at random restaurants in the area once a month just to catch up. We all made it out of this place, but it keeps us humble to have a monthly reminder of where we came from."

"Hmmm," I say non-committedly. He just winks at me in return.

We sit in silence until the limo gets to the Walmart parking lot that sits at the address I gave him. He looks out the window.

"I'm not leaving you here," he says firmly.

"I'm not letting you see where I live," I toss back at him in just as stern of a tone. "After all, you did wait for me outside of the diner for hours. That definitely qualifies you for scary stalker status."

He flashes me the first real smile I've seen on him and my heart involuntarily flutters. Stupid, traitorous heart.

"Does it lessen the stalker status if I tell you I went back to work until the time your friend said you would be getting off?" he asks.

I pretend to think about it.

"No, not at all," I tell him, opening the door out into the pouring rain before he can stop me.

Much to my dismay, or delight if I'm being truthful, he gets out behind me.

"I'll walk you then," he yells over the pounding rain.

I'm sure I look like a drowned cat by this point.

"Why are you here?" I finally ask, dismayed.

"What do you mean?"

"I mean, I clearly don't want anything to do with you. Why are you being so persistent? Is this some kind of game?"

He looks at me for a moment before answering.

"I've never seen someone so sad before," he says. "Something about you made it so that I couldn't leave you alone."

For some reason I'm crying. I'm grateful for the rain and the dark night because at least my tears won't be obvious to this infuriating stranger. Infuriating because I feel a pull towards him. A pull I am determined to avoid at all costs. I'm barely hanging on as it is. I'm literally always one step away from not being able to come back from the sorrow that is my constant companion. I won't survive one more time. I don't even know how I'm still standing right now.

"Please," I tell him, my voice choked with tears. "Leave me alone. There's no good ending to this story for either of us."

"You need a friend," he said. "I can be that for you. I won't ask for anything else."

"You'll fall in love with me," I tell him stubbornly and perhaps insanely.

"It's possible," he says with a wry grin. "But friends are allowed to be in love with each other. I believe it's called 'unrequited love.' There's quite a few books about it."

The words hang between us. What happens if I fall in love with him back?

"I just want to make sure you get home safely," he says softly, holding up his hands in front of him as he approaches me slowly, like I'm a wounded animal that could run away with any sudden movement.

I let him lead me back into the limo. I give him my address, and we sit silently for the rest of the trip. We're both soaking wet and I'm grateful for the heater as I had begun shivering shortly after we got back into the car.

We pull up to the battered apartment complex I call my home. His face pulls into a frown as he looks at it. Luckily for this friendship he's proposing, he says nothing. I may not have much, but I work hard for what I do have.

"Do you work tomorrow?" he asks, as I put my hand on the door handle to leave.

"I'm off," I say after a pause.

"There's a party..." he starts. "Very casual," he continues quickly when I start to shake my head automatically. "Just a few friends. You could meet people."

"How do you know I don't already know people," I say snottily.

"You can meet more people," he amends, although the look on his face says he knows I'm completely full of shit. Bethany is the closest I could call a friend, and she's old enough to be my mother...if we're counting the age I look and not the age I actually am.

"Pick you up at seven?" he asks.

We stare at each other for a long moment before I finally open the limo door and step back into the rain.

"Okay," is all I say before I walk towards my apartment.

I feel his eyes following me all the way to my door.

Keep reading Lamented Pasts, Book 1 of the Timeless Affection series here: https://amzn.to/2Vw4MqH

Read Lost Passions, Book 2 of the Timeless Affection Series here: https://amzn.to/2UGa2Le

Dive into a fantastical world of romance, alpha males, and kick ass heroines with book 1 in the Gods and Monsters series, Apollo Is Mine, from Mila Young.

APOLLO IS MINE SNEEK PEEK

I'm a warrior. Cursed to fight monsters. Sworn to act as Zeus' sword to protect mankind.

But I'd give it all up for one last kiss with the god who stole my heart...Apollo.

I never wanted to carry my family's legacy. But blood ties cannot be broken, and I'll keep the promise I made my father on his dying bed. Legendary monsters hunt in city streets of Chicago, and my job was to take down the worst.

I've trained with Heracles.

Been blessed with super human powers.

What I've never done is fallen in love—until Apollo crossed my path. But he isn't the only god to catch my attention. Hades is here too, and with him comes a darkness that leaves behind a trail of human bodies. Heracles and my gut instinct urges me to destroy this creature, but each step brings me closer to the truth...

Darkness cannot win...or the Earth will tumble into chaos and I'll lose the god I've come to love...Apollo is mine.

CHAPTER 1

Elyse

I spun and kicked back, aiming for the solar plexus. Heracles stepped out of the way, and with lightning speed, he was behind me, his arm around my neck. He squeezed until I couldn't breathe, my lungs stinging. Panic swirled in my gut.

I grabbed his arm with both hands and pulled down, curling my body into a ball. It threw him off-balance, enough for me to get out of his death grip and gasp for air. He redeemed himself in no time—he was a demigod, after all, and he didn't fall for the primitive moves of a mere human. I felt his power push down on me like a giant hand —not his physical strength, but the magic that came with his god side. It made it harder to focus as his magic gave off electrical sparks against my very essence.

But I wasn't fully human either. Once I harnessed the strength of the gods in me, I could hold my own in a fight. Most of the time. I reached deep and tugged at that line inside me that plugged me into Zeus directly. Yes, the king of the gods. The magic simmered beneath my skin like fire, and I pushed the invisible power at Heracles, slamming into him.

Eyes wide open, he staggered on the spot. Our energies crashed into each other, sending out a wave that knocked over the chairs in the corner of the empty Chicago community hall we fought in and sent them sprawling.

I used Heracles's arm, which I still held on to, and swung around, heaving myself up to land on his back, wrapping my legs around his torso as best I could. One arm was around his mouth and nose, the other around his throat. I had him.

Heracles didn't agree. Grunting, he fell backward, using his weight to pin me, and it forced all the air out of my lungs. I didn't let go of my grip, but Heracles had the upper hand now. Damn him. He rolled over, and somehow, his hands were on my shoulders, his knees on my legs, and I could do nothing but stare at his smirk.

"You're dead," he said in a low voice.

I groaned and squeezed my eyes shut. "I have more lives."

"Not infinite. You only have three. Don't waste them," he snarled.

Why had Zeus given my family a limit on how many lives we had while we fought gods and creatures that were close to impossible to defeat? My ancestors had been fighting evil on Earth for so long, no one remembered exactly how long ago Zeus had blessed us. While we were strong and had supernatural abilities, we could still die from injuries like normal humans, and then we awoke in the same body, age, and time we died... basically we'd survived death. But if we were lucky enough to die of natural old age, the catch was, we were dead forever. No being reborn with another life. Zeus had a funny sense of humor, apparently.

"That's not fair." I wriggled for release.

"It's never fair in the field. Do you think it was fair when I faced my twelve labors? No, but I overcame my fear and succeeded." He raised his chin in pride like he always did when he spoke of his achievements. Those sharp cheekbones gave him a chiseled look, and there was no denying he was handsome. But the demigod sure loved to brag.

"Elyse, you're smaller than I am in size," he continued. "You're smaller than any of the creatures or gods you're battling. So you have to fight smart," he insisted.

"Let me up," I rumbled.

Heracles released me, and I rolled over, panting. I hated whenever I lost to him during our training sessions. Which was often, considering he was powerful enough to take down gods. I hated the way he tried to hold back the grin each time. I hated that I still hadn't mastered my strength.

"I can't do this, Herc," I responded. "You're only a demigod, and I can't even beat you. What happens when my opponents are all magic without an ounce of humanity?"

Heracles frowned. "Thanks for that," he said sarcastically, shadows crowding under his eyes. "But I can take on any god, so if you beat me, you'll be ready to go."

"I didn't mean it that way. But our powers are more evenly matched. The other gods are bound to be stronger, right?" I had battled monsters before, but never a hostile god who intended to harm humans.

Heracles sighed loudly, running a hand through his sandy hair. "You can do this. My dad didn't choose your family for this task because he thought any of you were weak."

I shook my head. "Strength in numbers, remember? And where are those numbers? I'm the only one left." My voice climbed as my stomach hardened at the injustice of my family line appointed to protect humans from godly monsters, yet we weren't given the same abilities to battle them adequately. So everyone I loved had been killed in battle. I glanced down, blinking to push back the tears, reminding myself to slow my breaths. This wasn't Heracles's fault. He was the only one helping me.

My phone buzzed from inside my bag against the wall. I ignored it as Heracles kneeled in front of me where I sat on the foam mat. His eyes were cerulean blue, set in that Greek face of his. His nose was long and straight, his brows low, and he had the classic Greek olive skin that made everyone do a double-take. The humans knew Heracles was something else, but they could never put their fingers on it. It wasn't that he was built like an Adonis himself or he had eyes that made you shiver to your core. The gods all had something about them that made the humans fear them yet adore them at the same time.

Wasn't like I was in that category at all. Not even the slightest. I certainly didn't adore the gods. More like I had a love-hate thing going on with them. And the feeling was mutual at best. Zeus had given my family bloodline the power that ran through our veins as a birthright for generations. I was born of a lineage that had been chosen to fight the "Good Fight" here on Earth while these gods were busy with more important things on Mount Olympus. I snorted a laugh. Yeah right. But I was one of them, in a way.

"You've come a long way," Heracles stated, his voice sharp and authoritative. "Your father would be proud."

At the mention of my dad, a pang of sorrow shot into my chest. His death had been the most recent, and the open wound still smarted, burrowing deep. That hollowness reminded me how alone I was in the world. But I pushed the agony away. I couldn't let the tragedy that had haunted my family for centuries distract me while we trained. I didn't want Heracles to know it was a weakness. My father's death had left me with no one, and I was terrified of dying for real.

Didn't matter that I could come back three times before it was my final death. Yep, logic made no sense when it came to fear. It just bubbled in my chest like a bomb about to detonate each time I imagined myself dying. Maybe I'd seen too many people I loved lose their lives too soon...I don't know. But I wasn't ready to leave this world.

"I realize I'm better than I was, but do you think it's enough?" I stared into the bluest eyes for any sign of what he really thought.

Heracles folded his massive limbs until he was cross-legged like me. Somehow, it looked wrong. That formidable body in shorts and T-shirt was made for battle, not hanging out on the floor.

"It's only enough if you believe it is."

Right. It was all in my head. He reminded me of that all the time. And I felt good about myself when I fought. Most of the time, I could ignore the nagging fear that I wasn't good enough and drag out the ability that made me stronger, faster, more powerful than other humans.

"Let's stretch," he suggested.

I rolled my eyes, huffing. "I'm tired."

"You'll be sore tomorrow if you don't stretch. This is training one-oh-one. Don't be a baby." He brushed his light brown hair backward over his temples, looking like he'd just stepped out of a hairdresser, while I sweated.

I groaned.

He burst out in laughter, the sound savage and echoing around us. "Always the dramatic one."

I fake-punched him in the arm. "You can't talk."

When he cocked a brow, I climbed to my feet. "Let's get this over with."

When our training session ended, Heracles picked up his duffle bag and turned toward me with a smile. "Good session. See you first thing in the morning?"

After I nodded, he left the training center to head home. Heracles lived on Earth, even though he had earned his way back into Mount Olympus centuries ago. He preferred staying with the humans, seeing that his adoptive parents and his true love, Megara, had been human. It had all been so long ago, it was purely a myth to everyone now. But to Heracles, Earth felt like home, he'd once told me. To the point where he taught self-defense classes at the local gymnasium, became an adventure junkie, and even had a profile on Tinder. Not that he needed to, but he insisted on keeping his options open until he found someone he clicked with. Mind you, he'd been on over a hundred dates with women who fawned over him, yet he still turned them down. Personally, I didn't believe he was over Megara, and he searched for an elusive replacement who didn't exist.

We'd been training every day of the week and on the weekend for the past five months. Since losing my dad, I took this a lot more seriously and wished I had done so when he'd been alive.

For now, every day was the same. No breaks. I only kept track of the days because of my friend. And he helped me not just because of the promise to his dad but to ensure we had a fighting chance to protect innocents.

His routine was the same as mine. Or maybe mine was the same as his. He was always around to help me.

I climbed into my SUV and threw my gym bag onto the back seat. It landed next to the camera bag I always carried with me. I stared at the concrete community hall Heracles hired for a couple of hours every day. There were bars on the windows and weeds growing across the front yard, but this place offered the people a place of hope. Locals could hire it for boxing classes for kids, gymnastics, and yoga.

My legs were numb, and my heart rate was still elevated despite the cool-down session we'd had. My chest hurt, but that wasn't from fighting.

Heracles had brought up my dad because he'd wanted me to know that Ernest Lowe would have been proud of his only surviving child. But I wished he hadn't brought it up.

Dad had died a hundred and eighty-three days ago. His death was still fresh in my mind. My brothers had already been gone by then. My dad had fought the Aeternae near an old abandoned hospital alone, and they had gotten the better of him, taking his last life.

I hated Zeus for that. When Zeus had given us our power, given the Lowe family and all their descendants the ability to protect the Earth from Death, some gods had countered our attacks by sending us mythical creatures to battle. If we didn't, they would kill the humans, and the more souls Hades could gather, the more Death won out.

My father had told me about Death when I'd been a little girl. I used to sit around the table with my brothers, and my father would tell us about a being that was unlike anything else. He lived with Hades, almost as a second personality in his very skin, and to those who knew him, Death was merely known as X. He had a name, but to mention it was to summon him, and no one wanted to die before their time.

X was the one who'd sent the Aeternae, the Griffins, the Centaurs, and the Chimera for us to fight when he figured we were bored. Or when he was.

The Aeternae were rhino-like creatures with sawtooth bones on their heads with which they maimed and killed.

My father had been powerful. He had been one of the

strongest Lowes in existence, but it had been a case of numbers. There'd been too many Aeternae, and my mother and brothers had already long been dead. Anyone who married into the Lowe family, didn't get the three-life gift. It was a blessing passed down through blood.

I had been away for photography work in Fresno, real work, not just a cover. I still blamed myself for not being there to help him fight, no matter how much Heracles told me it wasn't my fault.

X hadn't been the one to take my father's soul when he'd died. None of us would belong to Hades once our time was up. When we died, we were taken to live with the other heroes of old in peace. It was the only thing that made my father's death a little more bearable, but the whole absolute of leaving behind Earth and everyone I knew terrified me.

Anyway, X hadn't been able to get his stinking fingers on my father's soul, and he didn't swim eternally in the River of Souls that Hades watched over in the Underworld. My family—all of them—were at peace.

So now I trained alone here on Earth, my only confidant and companion the demigod Zeus had appointed to train the Lowes, his task on Earth that would justify him not returning to Mount Olympus. Heracles had become a shoulder to cry on, a grief counselor after my father's death, and a friend. And I trained because it was in my blood and so my dad's death hadn't been in vain. I'd carry on what he'd died for.

My phone beeped again. I grabbed it from my gym bag and found a message from a client buying several of my photographs I'd taken of an old, torn-down building. Fantastic, it meant money to pay my rent. I backed the car out of the parking lot and drove to my apartment on a busy street with cars parked in every spot along the curb. Luckily,

I had reserved parking at the back of the building. There were no trees or shrubs on the sidewalk here. Only cement and concrete.

The sky was gray and lightning played across the heavens, but it wasn't going to rain, according to my weather app. There'd been a time when I remembered the world to be a sunnier place, but Chicago was mostly cloudy now. The sun barely made an appearance. They blamed it on global warming. I wasn't so sure it was that simple.

At home, I undid the long braid I always wore my hair in, stripped off my training clothes—sneakers, yoga pants, and fitness tank top—and climbed into the shower. The water ran through my hair and over my body, easing my sore muscles. Every week, I was getting stronger, my body fitter and more toned than it had ever been. When I looked in the mirror, I stared at a warrior. My dark hair offset my pale skin that was typical of a Lowe, and my father's honey-colored eyes were haunted and filled with rage. He was the only reason I still did all of this. Sometimes, I believed I was a fool for still fighting.

There were Lowes spread all over the Earth, but if they hadn't been killed, they'd abandoned the cause or hadn't been taught about it at all because their forefathers had refused to support the fight. Their powers had dwindled from disuse, and I was alone still pushing on. I would avenge my family if nothing else.

If I gave up, their deaths would be for nothing.

When I climbed out of the shower, I turned on the radio in my room. All the stations were filled with talking. There was no music, only a constant chatter. Struggling to follow the conversation, I turned it back off. The silence was better.

After drying my hair, leaving it loose over my shoulders, I made a quinoa salad with raw salmon on the side. I trained hard, and I ate right. I never drank. Power like mine and losing control when I was drunk was a terrible combination. My brother Seth had proved that before he'd died.

I sat down on the couch with my meal and switched on the television.

Someone knocked on my door, and I groaned. I didn't feel like getting up; plus, I was starving.

"Elyse," Heracles called. I recognized his voice through the door. I frowned. Heracles never came to my apartment.

I pushed myself up from the couch and hurried to the front door. When I opened it, Heracles stood there larger than life, his brow furrowed with concern. He wore the leather armor he was depicted wearing in all the images in books and on the internet, complete with the rubber wristbands, the leather strip skirt, and the sandals. He held the golden shield as if it were made of paper. A black strip was tied around his forehead, and his light chestnut hair was pulled back in a ponytail of sorts. He looked divine, to say the least. I lost my breath and was pretty sure my neighbors might die of shock at seeing him dressed up this way.

"Did you go see your dad? Or are you heading to a costume party?" I teased, hoping it was the latter since that meant this wasn't a serious talk. Or maybe for a change, he was inviting me out to have fun?

He stepped into the apartment, all shoulders and brooding. Worry knotted in my gut. I'd never seen him dressed like this. Supernatural energy radiated off him like steam, and I had to take a few deep breaths to steady myself.

"What's wrong?"

He arched an eyebrow as if my comment didn't warrant a response. "Yeah, I went to see Dad, and I'm here to warn you. Something big is coming." His velvety voice was deeper than usual. The more time he spent on Earth between visits to his dad, the more the god-quality wore off and he seemed more like a human. A perfectly sculpted, crazy attractive human, but still. When he came back from Mount Olympus, he was riddled with power that skipped down his arms.

"Like what?" I asked, not sure I was ready to press the panic button yet. He had a habit of over-worrying, like last month when he'd insisted I shouldn't visit the new café in town that had a peacock for its brand. I'd seen no issue with it, while he'd insisted the location was affiliated with Hera. Oh yeah, someone still held a grudge against the Queen of the Olympian gods, who believed peacocks were sacred. Then again, Hera had tricked Heracles into going mad and he killed his loved ones. Anyway, I'd visited the café and had the best coffee ever. Plus, I'd survived.

Heracles shifted his weight from one foot to the other, as if he struggled to stand in the afterglow of the gods, just like me. It buzzed in my veins, as if I'd eaten two big chocolate blocks in a row. And now, I hummed on a high.

"I don't know." Worry marred his brow. "My father warned me. Hades is causing trouble in the Underworld. Whatever is going to happen, it will probably come up from the Underworld. You have to be ready." He spoke fast, the bridge of his nose pinching.

Suddenly, fear clutched at my throat, and my chest was tight. "What if I'm not ready? This is freaking Hades we're talking about! I can't even defeat you!"

He stiffened, squaring his shoulders. "You have to be ready, Elyse. You're the only one left, and if something is coming and you don't do anything, a lot of people are going to die." He gripped his hips, staring down at me as if I were a child in the same way my dad used to do when I'd refused to train.

I closed my eyes and forced myself to breathe. I could do

this. Wasn't this what I'd been training for? Besides, I couldn't stand Hades, so whatever he sent our way deserved an ass-kicking.

But I hoped to God that Hades wasn't personally going to visit Earth. And this was why I so wished Heracles had said we were going to a costume party instead. Because if I was taking on the god of the Underworld on my own, I might as well sign my own death warrant right now.

Keep Reading Apollo Is Mine Here.

Jump into the rest of the Gods and Monsters series:
> **Poseidon Is Mine**
> **Ares Is Mine**
> **Hades Is Mine**

JOIN C.R.'S FATED REALM

Visit my **Facebook** page to get updates.

Visit my **Amazon Author** page.

Visit my **Website**.

Sign up for my **newsletter** to stay updated on new releases, find out random facts about me, and get access to different points of view from my characters.

OTHER BOOKS BY C.R. JANE

The Fated Wings Series

First Impressions

Forgotten Specters

The Fallen One (a Fated Wings Novella)

Forbidden Queens

Frightful Beginnings (a Fated Wings Short Story)

Faded Realms

Fearless Dreams (2019)

The Rock God (a Fated Wings Novella)

The Timeless Affection Series

Lamented Pasts

Lost Passions

The Pack Queen Series

Queen of the Thieves

Queen of the Alphas (2019)

Broken Souls Series

School of Broken Souls (2019)

The Rise Again Series

The Day After Nothing (2019)

The Sounds of Us Contemporary Series

Remember Us This Way

Remember You This Way

Remember Me This Way (2019)

Fallen World Series Co-write with Mila Young

Bound

Broken

JOIN MILA YOUNG'S WICKED READERS

Mila Young tackles everything with the zeal and bravado of the fairytale heroes she grew up reading about. She slays monsters, real and imaginary, like there's no tomorrow. By day she rocks a keyboard as a marketing extraordinaire. At night she battles with her might pen-sword, creating fairy-tale retellings, and sexy ever after tales. In her spare time, she loves pretending she's a mighty warrior, walks on the beach with her dogs, cuddling up with her cats, and devouring every fantasy tale she can get her pinkies on.

Join my **Facebook** reader group.

Visit my **Amazon Author** page.

Sign up for my **newsletter** for newest releases, exclusive excerpts, giveaways and loads of games.

BOOKS BY MILA YOUNG

Gods and Monsters

Apollo Is Mine

Poseidon Is Mine

Ares Is Mine

Hades Is Mine

Haven Realm Series

Hunted (Little Red Riding Hood Retelling)

Cursed (Beauty and the Beast Retelling)

Entangled (Rapunzel Retelling)

Wicked Heat Series

Wicked Heat #1

Wicked Heat #2

Wicked Heat #3

Elemental Series

Taking Breath #1

Taking Breath #2

Fallen World Series Co-write with Mila Young

Bound

Broken

Made in the USA
Monee, IL
25 April 2021